tricky WISDOM

Camryn Eyde

Tricky Wisdom: Year I
By Camryn Eyde

Cover design by Camryn Eyde

camryneyde.com

Authors Note

This is a piece of fiction, and while the greatest care has been taken to be as medically accurate as possible, I send my heartfelt apologies to any medically-trained readers at the off-chance I've mixed up the ileum with the ilium. I'm not a doctor, I've never been to medical school, and I'm certain I've grossly underestimated just how hard it is to train to become a physician. To those that have dedicated their lives to healing others, you have my utmost respect.

For
All the dedicated healers in the world

YEAR I

Chapter One

Perfect. She was just damn perfect.

I sighed and continued waving at the speck that was my best friend as the bus gained momentum. She had stood at the bus terminal in a summer frock that showed off all that olive skin that I longed to touch. Moving away was unavoidable. Studying to become a doctor was rather difficult in a town boasting a total population of one thousand. I sighed again and thought of Taylor's beatific smile. Of her twinkling blue eyes. Of those full, plump lips, I had been staring at since I was thirteen and wondering what they'd taste like.

I sighed, thinking of the night before when I had been given the perfect moment to tell my best friend how I felt.

"I wish you didn't have to go," Taylor had said, hugging me tight and stalling our progress to the lakeside docks.

"Me too," I said, hugging her back just as tight and mentally mapping the way her body fit against mine. For the millionth time, I cringed at myself taking advantage of moments like these. If Taylor knew, I was pretty sure all our public displays of platonic affection would cease to exist.

"I want to keep you here in my arms forever," she had whispered against my neck.

Goosebumps erupted across my body. "I want to stay here forever," I whispered back against the blonde hair falling down over her shoulders. I licked my lips, my mouth turning dry as I tried to work up the courage to tell her I'd been head over heels in love with her for years. "Tay, I…the thing is. I'm kind of…well…I…"

"You?" Taylor said, pulling back a little to look at me.

I chickened out, that's what I did. "I'll miss you."

She smiled and pecked me on the mouth in the one-thousand-two-hundred and twenty-first time. She had been my first kiss. My first closed-mouth, totally platonic, nothing is ever going to come from this kiss.

"I'll miss you too. Now, let's get to the bonfire. I bet Jack is there."

I rolled my eyes the moment she turned. Jack was the high school sweetheart that took her innocence in middle school. A milestone that felt like having hot pokers jabbed into my heart and ears. Jack was henceforth my mortal enemy. It was a shame he was the local doctor's son. A man I considered my hero.

"Yay," I muttered, unable to keep my disapproval from my voice.

"Careful, Darce, you're beginning to sound jealous." Taylor laughed over her shoulder.

Well, duh!

I sighed, bringing myself back to the present as the bus leaned into a corner. Last semester, I had completed my pre-med requirements and had applied with fingers crossed to Harvard University. I figured if I'm going to study to become a doctor, then I'm going to do it at the best university I could find. Thankfully, my undergraduate degree was completed with honors and my letters of recommendation from my state university had been overflowing with praise. A tense few months, lots of exams, and some nail biting as I waited for my MCAT scores, plus a long-winded letter pleading for financial aid later, here I was on the way to Boston with a rigorous four years ahead of me. I couldn't help sighing…again.

"Careful, dear."

I looked to Mrs. Henderson sitting across the aisle from me. "Pardon?"

"All that sighing. It'll give you an aneurysm."

As a pre-med student, I knew that was a bunch of hokum, but I smiled and nodded at her anyway.

"Besides, how can someone as young as you have such weighty matters getting them down?"

"I'm just going to miss home. First time away and all that."

Mrs. Henderson raised her painted-on eyebrows at me. "Fibs will clog your arteries."

"What?"

"If memory serves, this is, in fact, your sixth time away from home."

I blinked. Mrs. Henderson, the town know-it-all, was right. Scout camp, that time we visited a dying relative, and the trips to university for my undergrad. "Well, this is the first time I'm going away with no intention of coming back for months. Maybe years."

Mrs. Henderson nodded in understanding. "Very well, dear."

Thinking that was the end of it, I went back to watching the countryside zip past the window on the way to the St. Paul Airport in Minneapolis. Mrs. Henderson had other ideas. Considering we were the only two on the bus, discounting Gus, the driver, her need to chatter was solely my problem.

"You must be diligent in the city, dear," she told me at the start of a very long lecture about miscreants, deviants, insurgents intent on ruining civilization, and your common everyday criminal out to steal a young woman's virtue. We just passed the airport welcome sign when she finished her six-hour story. "... and that's when Dorothy thought she saw her late husband's ghost. Right there, standing on the porch as if he was coming home from the mines."

Tuning back in on the last sentence, I stared at her agape. "Huh?"

"Dorothy, dear."

I nodded and made a humming noise as if I completely understood her inane ramblings. "We're here," I said, distracting her from frowning at me.

"Oh, yes. We are. Now, remember, dear, stay away from ghosts, gypsies and politicians. Remember what happened to Dorothy and you'll be fine."

"Ah…you betcha."

Harvard pre-med. One of the most competitive and daunting schools I could think of, and that was downright scary enough. Even more worrisome was discovering the apartment you were barely able to afford a room at was occupied by a roommate with a serious personality disorder.

Olivia Boyd entered my life with a sneer and disapproving blue eyes raking over my casual, country-girl look. She was taller than me by a four-inch margin, she was also slimmer, which was difficult to achieve. My metabolism made my eating habits the envy of everyone I knew. Olivia wore a professional look. Her dark hair was pulled back into a messy-but-trendy bun and the wisps fell gently on narrow shoulders. I envied her hair instantly. Mine was dark as well, but growing length was challenging, so I kept it just long enough to scrape into a tiny ponytail.

She crossed her arms over a gray vest and a crisp white shirt. Grey trousers completed the look as they descended to the ground to heel-clad feet. That explained her height. Without those shoes, she'd be a good two inches shorter.

"And you are?" she said, distaste in her words. I couldn't decide whether it was because of my presence, or the fact I just assessed her clothing.

"I'm Darcy," I said, holding out my hand for her to take. She sneered at it.

"And you're studying at Harvard?"

"Yes."

Her lip curled. "As what?"

I furrowed my brow. "Pardon?"

"Are you one of those charity cases universities take on from time to time?"

"Charity case? No."

She hummed.

I shook my head at her and inspected the rooms I had blindly signed my life over to for the next few years. The place wasn't large. In fact, I could see the entirety of it from my position by the front door. Olivia stood just to my side at the entrance to the pokey kitchen. In front of us was a four-chair table, a two-seater sofa surrounding an outdated entertainment system and a small balcony giving us a view of the city from our third floor. Turning my head away from Olivia, I could see two large desks placed against the walls in the space between the doors to the bedrooms and bathroom.

"My room is the one on the left."

I shrugged. I didn't care where I slept. "Are you taking the left desk, too?" I asked, picking up my suitcase and entering my new room. The single bed took up most of the space, and a closet and night table completed the bedroom ensemble.

"Yes," Olivia said, answering my question.

Dumping my bag, I returned to the living area and looked at the place I would most likely be sitting for the majority of the next few years. The desk was old and marred with dents, etched initials of past students and random lines of ink from wayward pens. Coffee stains had replaced the varnish that once existed on the table top.

"So…" I said with a long exhale. "What are you studying?"

"Pre-med," Olivia said curtly.

"What did you major in?" I said, referring to the undergraduate degree she had to have taken to apply in the first place.

"Biochemistry."

Impressed, I nodded. "I stu—"

She held up a hand. "I'm not interested in whatever humanitarian program got you here. I can only assume you're going to be commuting to and from the main campus. Which, if I'm honest, makes your decision to live south of the river an astonishing one."

I shrugged. "I like living on the wild side."

She sneered. "Yes, well, considering that, I have something that will assure our time in this apartment will go smoothly."

"Oh?" She produced a thick document and handed it to me. I read the term *Roommate Agreement* on the cover. "Seriously?"

"Very." She indicated for me to sit in the lounge space with her.

"You watch too much TV."

She looked offended. "I abhor television."

"Then what's with this Sheldon book," I said, tapping the document in my hand.

"Who's Sheldon?"

I gave her my best are-you-serious look. "Big Bang Theory," I offered as a clue.

She looked confused. "I'm sorry, I have no interest in the theories of astrophysics."

"What? That's not...never mind." I rubbed my temple and tried to ease the ache forming there.

"This document, something I downloaded from the internet I'll have you know, ensures a harmonious living environment. Essentially, it's an agreement to respect each other's space, need for quiet study, and to ensure our living space stays as clean as possible."

I flicked through the novel. It looked like jargon to me.

"My program of study is rigorous, and requires a significant amount of dedication. Unlike yourself, I have no time to waste on trivialities such as a social life."

I shook my head at her second assumption that I was here doing social sciences or some other arts-like degree. I preferred to keep her clueless and planned to savor the look on her face when I turned up in all her classes.

She handed me a green piece of paper. "Here's a list of addendums."

"Of who-what?"

"Addendums. My preferences for a roommate that ensure I have a quiet residence to complete my MD."

I scanned her list.

No television in my presence.

No music of any sort – use headphones.
No visitors. Relatives included.
No significant others.
No gossip and inane conversation.
Cell phones to remain on mute within the house.
Refrain from utilizing my food.

The list continued down the page.

"You're kidding, right?"

"I don't kid."

"Yeah, that I can tell." I huffed and tossed the paperwork to the coffee table. "I'm not signing that."

"You must."

"No, I mustn't." I stood and stretched. "I'm not a slob. I respect other people, and I have no friends or significant others to invite here. My phone doesn't have an obnoxious ringtone. I don't watch much television, and I love my headphones. I'm here to study, not to party."

She rose to look me in the eye. "Very well, then. Perhaps this documentation is unnecessary."

Hell, yes, it is. I hummed a response and went to the kitchen in search of a snack. The fridge was stocked with a ton of fresh food. None of it mine. "You cook?" I asked as I stared at the ingredients in there. Some completely foreign.

"Of course I do."

I scoffed to myself. I bit my lip in thought. I couldn't cook worth a damn, and nor could I afford take out every day. I had planned on surviving on noodles for the next few years regardless of all the hype about them being coated in plastic. I shut the fridge door with a sigh. "Where's the local grocery store?"

"Depends. Are you interested in a 7-Eleven or a market that sells actual food?"

"I'm not fussy."

"Of course you aren't. The 7-Eleven is a left at the main street, and a selection of whole food markets are to the right, then south near the animal center."

"Okay." I went to my room and changed into my favorite running clothes and shoes. I figured I may as well explore the area by foot. Not that I had a choice. The only transportation I had here was walking or bus. Strapping my phone to my arm and selecting some tunes, I yelled out a goodbye to an unpacking roommate and headed for the store.

My phone rang before I got there. Taylor's name and picture lit up my screen. Smiling, I answered. "Hi!"

"Hello, city girl. How's the big smoke?"

I looked around my part of Boston. "Grey."

Taylor laughed. "So was Minneapolis."

"True." Smiling, I remembered spending the past four years at college with Taylor. We had rented an apartment off-campus for our time there. I barely saw her considering my workload and her need to party all the time. Gaining an MBA at the end of her study so she could run her father's store, she had also gained several notches on her bedpost in the process. Something I grimaced into the phone at. Those men were never right for her.

"You settled in then?" she asked.

"Mostly. Just on the way to the store. I met my roommate though…ugh."

"That good, huh?"

"She's like Sheldon. Came at me with a roommate agreement and everything."

Taylor laughed into the phone.

"She thinks I'm a hippy, or some country-hick wanting to know more about cows or something."

Taylor's laugh kept filling my ears. I loved her laugh. It was so carefree and light. I sighed and immediately thought of Mrs. Henderson and her aneurysm advice.

"Damn. Dad's calling me. Now that summer holidays are over, he's got it in his head that because I have an MBA, it's time to apply it. Ugh. Lame-o Daddy-o."

I smiled. "We're twenty-three, I don't think we're allowed to say things like lame-o daddy-o anymore."

"Says who?"

"Me. It sounds stupid."

She blew a raspberry down the phone. A male voice in the background yelled out for her and threatened consequences if she didn't hurry. "Ugh. If lame-o daddy-o sounds stupid, then I suggest you go and tell my dad that I'm too old to be grounded." She huffed. "I have to go. We're interviewing for a new store manager today."

"Enjoy."

She made a noise of dissent. "Love you."

"Me too." I sighed again when the call ended. I'm *in* love with you rattled around my head. Putting my phone away, I slumped the rest of the way to the store and stocked up on artery-clogging noodles, chips, and pastries. My heart already ached, so I figured I may as well tip it over the edge.

Chapter Two

Harvard Medical School was an easy stroll from our apartment. And by easy, it was less than a mile away. It was the reason I chose the cheap but worn-out apartment in the first place. I assumed Olivia leased it from whoever owned it and was the one to put out the advertisement for a roommate. Shaking my head, I couldn't fathom why she even wanted a roommate to begin with. She was asinine.

She also left incredibly early.

Our first class was at nine in a building I had yet to locate. Strolling down Longwood Avenue admiring the buildings around me, I managed to find the right one. Smiling, I made my way inside and followed my fellow straggling wannabe doctors into the auditorium.

"Ah, my last ducks," the professor said from the podium. "Come now, we've much to discuss and only two weeks to discuss it in. Hurry. Hurry."

I gave the man an odd look and quickly found a seat. I grinned as I spotted Olivia staring at me from the seated students with an incredulous expression. I added a little finger wave to my grin making her scowl and force her attention back to the professor at the front.

"I'm Dr. Allen, and I'm going to give a number of seminars with you fine young men and women this year. First off, I'd like in introduce our course facilitator who will give you a run down on the path to medical greatness."

A sour-looking woman emerged from the shadows. "Students," she said by way of address. "Congratulations on being the first intake to Pathways, a bold new approach to making you all the best doctors you can be. From now until Christmas, you will begin the pre-clerkship required to move into clinical experience and advanced clinical experience in year two and three. You will cover the foundations of biochemistry, genetics, biology, anatomy, histology, pathology, and so on. Next year, you'll have two more intensive blocks to survive. It's rigorous, and I expect you all to succeed. Fail, and your life in medicine just took a fatal hit." She clapped her hands together and made everyone jump. *Yikes.* "Year two of Harvard Medical, just got real people. No longer will students be coddled through classrooms and pandered to like children. Instead, you'll be thrown into what strengthens the backbone of any decent MD and transition straight into clinical experience. Here you learn how to become doctors, and those of you who manage to make it through the first year, will suffer and sweat. Your ranks will be culled as those that can't make the grade fall away. Trust me, there will be many. Maybe half of you will find yourselves in year three to take Step One exams…if you're lucky." She followed this delightful reality check with a dressing down about how lovely it was for us to dedicate our lives to help others, but dare we lose focus for a moment, then death and destruction will haunt our lives. It was quite the motivational speech. I considered taking up a degree in the arts as she waved her goodbyes and left us stunned and shaken.

Dr. Allen returned with a beaming grin. "Now…let's begin." He clicked a button and the projector screen at the front of the hall was lit up with the title: *Introduction to the Profession.*

The remainder of the day went by in a cloud of what life was like in the medical profession. It was dull with a smattering of points of interest. More interesting was my altercation with Olivia as we took a break for lunch.

She came at me hissing and spitting. "You!"

"Hi." I smiled and gave her another wave before rummaging around in my bag for money. "Are you getting lunch?"

"Why are you here? If this is some kind of prank, then I'll have you know, I'm not amused."

"I'm thinking a sandwich. What about you?"

She shook her head to clear her confusion. "What?"

"Lunch."

She blinked.

"Want some?"

She straightened as she finally fathomed my question. "I've something prepared. Now—"

"Where are you going to eat it? Let me grab something from the deli and I'll meet up with you, then you're more than welcome to continue interrogating me about why I'm here. Right now, though, I'm starving."

"I...I shall wait here." She indicated to the low stone wall beside us.

"Not really that comfortable, though, is it? How about I meet you over there on the grass?"

She looked to the quadrangle I pointed to. "You want me to sit on the ground?"

"Feel free to stand. Back in a moment." I hurried to find a sandwich and soda, and returned to see her awkwardly staring at the ground. "It doesn't bite."

"Ants do."

Good point. I inspected the area for ants. "None here. Sit already."

She scowled at the ground again and ripped a piece of paper from her notepad before delicately sitting on it.

"Comfortable, your royal highness?"

"No. Now, quit avoiding my question. Why are you here?"

"To study medicine. You?" I added sarcastically.

"You're pre-med?"

"Yes."

She made a harrumph noise in her throat that made me want to chuckle. I thought better of it. "I...didn't expect that."

"You didn't really ask."

"Yes, well..." she pulled a container from her bag and began to pick at a salad she had prepared. "I suppose your chosen field should at least make you appreciate the need for quiet study at the apartment. I suspect you will require ample amounts of it."

I washed a bite of the sandwich down with carbonated sweetness. "Is that your way of saying you think I'm stupid?"

She shrugged and speared a green leaf.

"I graduated with honors, I'll have you know, *and* was accepted for a scholarship here based entirely on my academic record."

She shrugged again. "Big deal. Several of us were."

I rolled my eyes to the heavens.

"What did you major in?" she asked after murdering more foliage.

"Biochemical engineering." The fork paused halfway to her mouth and I smirked. "What? Expecting some humanitarian endeavor?"

She put her fork down. "Frankly, yes."

"Surprise," I said in a sing-song voice. She scowled. Chuckling, I finished my lunch and we returned to our lecture.

∞

Day two and my wannabe-doctor status got more official. Sitting through dignitaries and formal introductions, one by one we made our way to the front of the auditorium to receive our white coats. Draping it over my shoulders was the head of the cardiothoracic clinic at the hospital down the road, and she looked severe, drained of life, and utterly fed up with it all. It gave me pause. Was torturing myself for four years going to be worth it if I came out the other end looking like my soul had been sucked out of my nose?

"Good luck. You'll need it," she said before giving away a white coat to the last of our group. Stellar advice.

She was right. From that day forward, I was nose-deep in books, sleep-deprived and functioning solely on caffeinated drinks.

Columbus Day arrived and we were into our third first-year subject. Two exams were over and I was having a lazy weekend to celebrate having survived the past seven weeks. Olivia didn't approve and was waving her arms around at me frantically. Pulling the headphones from my ears, I said, "What?"

She growled. "My decision to partner with you was obviously a mistake. I should have realized this earlier."

"What are you going on about?"

"We have patient-doctor sessions this week, and what are you doing? Goofing off! How are we supposed to plan an attack if you're lolling about on your backside?" She stormed to the kitchen and ripped a sparkling water from the fridge door. "Thank God this is individually assessed."

I shook my head and put my ear plugs back in. I added panic-prone to her list of quirks I had noted for her. I smiled as I checked them off in my head. *Paranoid. Obnoxious. Tetchy. Narcissistic. Snob. OCD. Anal. Tall. Meticulous. Freak.* The last one was added yesterday when she declared that chocolate was horrendous and she avoided it entirely. Anyone that avoids chocolate without a suitable medical reason was a freak in my book. I leaned over and reached for the beer I had retrieved ten minutes ago and took a long gulp. I raised the bottle to Olivia in salute as she curled her lip at me. Drinking when it was still daylight out also bugged her.

I stared over at the TV that was currently on mute and televising the Vikings game. Considering they were from my home state, I cheered quietly for them, but the score predicted a thrashing by our mortal enemy, the Green Bay Packers. I grunted as the Packers scored another touchdown.

My ear plugs were ripped from my ear a moment later. "Ow! What the hell!"

"You are interrupting my studies with your constant groaning and grunting. If you're not going to participate in learning, then have the decency to remain silent!"

I growled in frustration and flopped back to the couch. "Seriously, Ollie, it's Sunday, give it up for a moment."

"Ollie?" she said with a weird screech.

"Short for Olivia. What? Would you prefer Liv? Livvy?" The look on her face suggested she'd prefer an enema. "Ugh. *Olivia*, please, it's Sunday afternoon, we've been studying for seven weeks straight, sit down and chill."

She glared and yanked her anatomy book from the desk. Seeing that book made me itch inside. We'd met out first cadaver a few weeks ago, and the experience was forever etched into my mind. I was standing near Olivia when the groups were being decided, and was grouped together with her, George 'Tick' Harrison, Peter Howard, and Jane Delvine. Our cadaver was a sixty-three-year-old I secretly dubbed Dolores. We weren't really supposed to name the donor bodies, but I'll be damned if I was going to refer to this extraordinary person as donor one-two-five-one-F. It was too impersonal.

Olivia loomed over me and made me forget the itch. "I prefer to utilize my time wisely instead of watching the Vikings get smashed by the Packers...again." She paused at the door and smirked at me. "Go Big Bay Blues."

She shut her door, leaving me blinking at it in amazement. *She was a Green Bay Packer fan?* "Ugh! Typical," I muttered as I lay back on the couch, semi-impressed that she knew the sport. I added *arch enemy* to my list. Vikings fans had to hate Packers fans on principle. Good thing Olivia was a bona fide bitch.

With Olivia gone, I pulled the headphones from my ears and turned the volume up on the TV. Cheering quietly as we scored an answering touchdown to bring the score margin to sixteen, my cell rang.

"Hi. Are you watching the game?" I said, answering it.

"No. I'm at work. How we doing?"

"Don't ask."

"I hate the Packers."

"Ditto. Turns out Olivia is a fan, though."

Taylor laughed. "Not surprised. How is Olivia-the-weird going?"

I smiled at the nickname Taylor decided worked for my roommate. "She's panicking about our patient assessments this week. I'm partnered with her, so she just gave me a big lecture about lazing about in front of the game."

"That's because you're wasting my time," Olivia said from behind me. Startling, I jumped and spilled beer all over me after reaching for a sip.

"Jesus."

Olivia smirked at me and retrieved the drink she had forgotten before returning to her room.

"Damn it."

"What?" Taylor asked.

"I spilled beer. Such is my life at the moment."

"You could always come home. I miss you."

I stopped wiping the beer and smiled. "I miss you, too."

"Besides…I need my wing-woman back."

My smile fell away and my heart sunk. Taylor was on the prowl. "Oh?" I said, trying to sound interested.

"The new manager we hired…I think…" she sighed. "I might be in love."

I rolled my eyes and shook my head at Taylor's standard line when she found herself attracted to anyone. Wishing she'd say that to me one day, I asked, "Gorgeous?"

"You have no idea."

"Tall?"

"Yes."

"Let me guess…blue eyes and blonde hair?"

"No, actually." That gave me pause. Taylor never went for the dark guys. She had a thing about stubble shadow. "Brunette with chocolate-colored eyes. A bit like yours, actually."

Hearing myself referenced against someone Taylor was attracted to was a first, and I felt my stomach flop.

"Charli reminds me of you in a lot of ways."

I blinked. This was new. Very new. "Oh?"

"Which makes me miss you so much more."

I sighed into the phone. "I love you," I whispered, realizing that sounded a lot like longing.

"I know," she whispered back. Next second, she said brightly, "So...plan of attack. Do I sweep in with the flirting and innuendo, or play it cool and aloof?"

I shook my head. "I have no idea. I'm not sure what this guy is like. I can't help you."

"Umm...the thing is, you can. Charli isn't a guy."

I did what I could to stop that trickle of dread heading for my toes, but it was hopeless. "What?"

"Charli is a she. I'm falling for a woman."

Dread smashed every limb on its path around my body and into my heart. *She was attracted to a woman? Taylor?* My breathing shortened.

"Darcy?"

I swallowed. Hard. "W-why do you think I can help? I'm not..." *Not what?* I thought to myself. *Not willing to participate in letting another female take what was rightfully mine, that's what.*

"Oh," Taylor said. "God, I'm so sorry, I thought you were...you know?"

"What?"

"Umm...man this is awkward," she said in a rush.

"What is?"

"Aren't you gay?"

She knew? "What?"

Taylor groaned. "I knew I shouldn't have listened to Jack."

"Jack?"

"Yeah. He said the other week that you were...God...in love with me or something. What a prick, right?"

"Mmm."

"I just figured he was onto something, you know? Like, seriously, you've never had a boyfriend, or kissed anyone, so

I thought that maybe, umm, you were into the ladies but were too afraid to say, or something?"

I tried to unravel her sentence. Now or never, Darcy. Now or never. "I'm a lesbian," I said, proudly stating those words aloud for the first time in my life. *Go me.*

"I knew it."

I screwed my forehead up. *What sort of reaction was that?*

"Damn. Sorry, Darce, I have to dash. Can I call you later? You know, for advice?"

"I…umm, sure."

"Great. Bye."

The phone call ended and I was left feeling very anti-climactic about my coming out. Letting a 'this sucks' noise erupt in my throat, I stood to collect another beer only to find Olivia behind me staring at the TV. "Holy crap."

She turned her attention to me. "The TV sound is on. Could you please turn it down?"

I nodded and wondered if she'd overheard my phone call. I pre-empted she did and said, "Yes, I'm a lesbian."

She raised an eyebrow at me. "Good for you."

Okay, that reaction threw me as well. What was with coming out these days? Where was the drama, the understanding, the ticker-tape parade? No…scratch that one. That was just stupid.

"I'm bisexual."

I blinked. "What?"

"Since we're sharing sexualities, I figured I should offer mine."

"You're gay, too?"

"No, I'm *bisexual.*"

I frowned. To me, that sounded like she liked women, too, so wouldn't that make her gay? She rolled her eyes at my obvious confusion.

"It basically means I fall for the person, not the gender. Unlike some, I don't discriminate. Now, please turn that down. I can hear the inane ramblings through my bedroom door."

I snatched the remote and nearly pushed the mute button through the casing. I can't believe admitting I was a lesbian just got me insulted for excluding a gender from my preferences. I decided to add *bigoted wench* to my list.

Sulking, I sat back on the couch and downed the remainder of my six-pack as I watched the Vikings receive a sound thrashing. Today was about as bad as it could get. My team lost. I was arguing with my roommate...nothing new there, and my best friend that I had crushed after obsessively since junior school had decided to leap the fence and fall for some lookalike. I let out a shrieking growl and promptly ignored Olivia's chiding.

ॐ

"It's not fair," I whispered. I'm sure I heard Olivia's teeth grinding. "*I'm* the one that loves her, not this *Charli* ring-in. Ugh!"

I heard Olivia's hiss before she said, "For Pete's sake, will you please shut up."

I slumped forward and tapped my pen on my notepad. The lecturer up front was droning on about the causes of health disparities overseas. A hand suddenly clamped down hard over my tapping pen. I hissed in pain.

Olivia leaned in close, her bared teeth looking ready to go for my jugular. The two-inch gap between those perfect teeth and my pulsing lifeline made me nervous. "I do not care about your pathetic love life and its considerable faults. If you want this insipid *Taylor* so badly, then please don't let me stop you from high-tailing it home like the pitiful fool you are. In fact, do the world, and me, a favor and leave."

"Ladies? Do we have a problem?" the professor snapped us both back to attention.

"No, sir," Olivia said. I shook my head.

"Then perhaps, you wouldn't mind offering a three-point summary of my argument."

Olivia's jaw worked up and down in shock.

I huffed. "I believe, sir, that you were arguing that health stratification has several fundamental causes relating to education, employment, and poverty, as well as relating to welfare programs each country has in place. However, I'd like to argue that in some countries, affluence has less to do with health, than it has to do with the availability of services and eligible access to them. Population density, for example, thins the service on the ground regardless of payment ability. Additionally, some political agendas exclude people from health care access."

The professor coughed, or perhaps choked, and nodded sharply. "Thank you…?"

"Darcy Wright, sir."

"Darcy. Thank you for that succinct wrap-up. However, please refrain from gossiping in my class again."

I smiled and nodded. "No problem." Glancing at Olivia afterward, I saw an expression of pure shock. In fact, she looked immobilized. "Hey," I said quietly, careful not to attract the professor's attention again. I nudged her with my elbow which got a response.

She blinked at me, shook her head and refused to acknowledge me for the rest of the lecture.

∞

"You're intelligent," she said to me in what sounded like accusation when we returned to the apartment. We'd taken to walking back together as the days grew shorter. I called it roommate bonding, she labeled it safety. Apparently my diet and its effect on my heart would hinder my ability to outrun her if chased by criminals. I was bait.

"Umm…I try to be. Why?"

"How…you…" she narrowed her eyes at me. "Have you been reading my notes?"

"Trust me, Liv, I wouldn't dare."

"*Olivia.*"

I ignored her correction and headed to my room to change. I wanted to catch a run before the sky darkened any further. Besides, I ran out of pizza. I had to do a grocery store. Inspecting my wallet before leaving my room, I winced. My student salary was abysmal, and my inability to cook was straining my bank account. Wondering if I should ask Mom and Dad to sell my car back home and provided me with some sort of income, I shrugged it off. I worked hard to earn that Mustang, as rusty and junk-worthy as it was. I needed to find work. This made me deflate. *Like I had time to add work to my schedule.*

"Going out," I called through the bathroom door as I left.

"Wait!" Olivia poked her head out, shoulders bare and a towel wrapped around her. "I need…what?"

Snapping out of my instant need to stare, I pointed to her shoulder. "You have a tattoo." *And really nice clavicles,* my anatomy-fixated mind produced. I smiled at myself.

She looked suspicious. "It's just a tattoo, not a national secret," she said, misinterpreting my look. Perhaps she thought I was going to blackmail her with its existence.

"What is it?" I asked, stepping closer. She flinched.

"An owl."

"Why?" I peered at it and saw a small owl in flight high on her upper arm.

"Wisdom."

"Or a Harry Potter freak."

She fidgeted and I saw a blush move up her neck. Fascinating as that was to witness, I put two-and-two together. "Seriously? You have a Hedwig tattoo?"

"Hedwig is white, you imbecile. This is Pigwidgeon. Ron's owl."

I grinned. "Dork."

"Ugh!" She turned and slammed the door of the bathroom in my face. "I need feta cheese. Please get me some while you're out pretending to improve your cardiovascular fitness."

Making a face at the door, I left without responding. Running along the street a short while later, I burst into a fit of giggles. Olivia was a Potter-head. I instantly added that to her list. That and skeptical. There was no way anyone could pretend to run. Puffing and panting as I arrived at the 7-Eleven, I double-over and forced air into my lungs. Running sucked, but it certainly wasn't pretend. Unsure that my cardiovascular strength was being improved or compromised, I found some feta cheese and frozen pizza before jogging back home and swigging from a soda bottle. All this exercise hopefully negated my woeful, non-medically approved diet.

I had to stop to wipe soda from my top as I misjudged my coordination and ended up staring at a Help Wanted sign. I stepped back and looked at the name of the business. *Sunny's Dry Cleaning*. I bit my lip and stepped closer to the door. Cupping my hands, I peered inside. It was dark. I made a mental note to come back tomorrow to ask.

&

I burst into the apartment after scaling the stairs like a champion and Olivia yelped.

"Sorry."

"Must you be so Neanderthal?"

"Yup." I shoved the feta in the fridge and tossed my pizza in the oven. Olivia was grimacing when I turned back around. "What?"

"Pizza, again?"

I shrugged. "So?"

"You're studying to become a doctor, yet you insist on clogging your arteries on a daily basis."

"They're my arteries to clog. Why do you care?"

"I don't, except for the fact that junk food of yours smells revolting. Ever thought to actually *cook* something edible?"

I sniffed and scratched behind my ear. "Not really. I can't cook."

Olivia frowned at me. "Is that why you constantly fill your body with rubbish?"

"Pizza has vegetables on it. And dairy. It's not all rubbish."

"It's refined flours and carbs. It's vile and fit only for rats."

"I don't have pizza all the time. Sometimes I order Chinese."

"Which contains a bevy of preservatives and questionable meats."

I shrugged. I didn't care. It filled the hole in my stomach.

Olivia stormed over to the oven, pulled out my pizza and threw it in the bin.

"Hey! That's my dinner...and breakfast. Lunch, too, probably," I said, trailing off morosely. I felt like I was about to cry. I was starving.

"I refuse to smell burnt cheese and fried fat again. You are going to learn how to cook."

"I what?"

"You heard." Olivia scribbled down something on a scrap of paper and handed it to me. "Fetch these ingredients."

Eyes wide, I felt my slightly clogged heart pound erratically. "I can't."

"Yes, you can."

"No, I mean, I can't afford to. Not until Thursday."

Olivia huffed. "Fine." Opening the fridge, she yanked out eggs, ham, and some green leafy things. "Come here. You're making an omelet."

I cringed.

Half an hour later, I patted my stomach and sighed happily. "That was amazing. Thank you."

Olivia smiled and tipped her head in my direction. "You're welcome."

"I can't believe I made that."

"Proves that anything is possible."

"Har-har." I picked up our empty plates and started the dishes. Considering she just showed me how to feed myself, it was the least I could do. After putting the last dish away, I approached her carefully with the plan I had been formulating while my hands were in the soapy water. "Umm…"

She cocked her head at me as she looked up from her textbook. "Yes?"

"You know how to cook."

"Yes."

"I don't."

She scoffed in agreement.

"Will you cook for me?"

Her eyebrows smacked into her forehead. "Excuse me?"

"I, umm, well…I'll contribute to the food and wash up after."

"While I act as your personal chef?"

"No, not *exactly*." I groaned and sat in the chair at my study desk and looked over to Olivia. "Okay, maybe that is what I'm asking. Maybe you can teach me some stuff? Enough so I can cook more than omelets and then I'll leave you alone."

"And what, exactly, do I get from this?"

"A personal dishwasher?"

"And?"

"Umm…" I scratched at my eyebrow. "I'll clean the bathroom for the rest of the school year."

She leaned back in her chair and crossed her arms, looking interested, but not convinced.

"I'll stop drinking straight from the milk bottle."

Her face contorted to one of disgust. "You drink straight from the bottle?"

"No." I looked anywhere but at her horrified expression. "Of course not. I was just saying that, *if* I did, I'd stop."

"Damn right you'll stop." She shuddered in revolt. "Fine," she snapped a moment later. "You have bathroom duty, *weekly* bathroom duty, dishwashing duty, *and* you'll stop being a repulsive wretch with my milk."

I grinned, victorious and enthusiastic about being nutritionally proactive. "Awesome. Thanks." I dashed across the space between us and hugged her spontaneously. She was like hugging a plank. All stiff and splintery.

"You will also never do that again," she said when I pulled away.

"You betcha." I winked at her, earning an eye roll.

Chapter Three

I scored the job at Sunny's Dry Cleaning, and subsequently spent half of my weekends, and two weeknights trying not to identify the stains on the clothes I was handling. My study time plummeted by sixteen hours each week, and I felt like my doctor portion of my brain was being replaced with trying to remember what solvents matched what stain. Pre-treatment, hydrocarbon solvent ratios, post-spotting techniques, pressing and folding—it was all I could think about. I took that as necessary collateral damage for my new-found ability to afford what Olivia called *proper* food, and discovered I had managed to save some of it too. I spent that savings the instant it reached the amount that would buy me a return ticket home for Thanksgiving. Mom's turkey was an institution, and I deserved the reward after months of classes, study, working and living off zero sleep.

Thanksgiving approached with a hurry. Halloween, my all-time favorite holiday of the year, came and went with a minimum amount of decoration in the apartment. All I got away with thanks to the Scrooge McDuck of Halloween was a picture of a carved pumpkin on my door. I made up for the lack of decorations with candy. A lot of candy. As I studied for my practical exam in anatomy, I was still crunching on my abundant supply of Reese's peanut butter bites. Each time I crunched, Olivia, who was working diligently at the desk beside me, stiffened and rolled her shoulders. I did my best to chew quietly lest she tossed my booty in the bin.

"Tell me," I said, interrupting the silence. "What happens during each step of the myosin-actin cross bridge cycle?"

Olivia glanced over at me and frowned. I assumed she was thinking. "Are you serious?"

I nodded and sucked on another Reese.

She huffed at me. "Fine." Taking a breath, she was about to answer when my phone rang. A Britney Spears hit sounded through the apartment.

"Hang on," I said, holding up a finger. Olivia scowled as I answered. "Taylor, how are you?"

"Hey there, stranger. I'm great. I'm in love. Your tips worked."

My face fell in an instant. Eventually advising my friend to be aloof and non-responsive to Charli were supposed to turn the woman off, not make her catch the woman I loved. "Oh?"

Olivia rolled her eyes. "Let me guess, your imaginary lover ran off with the store girl?" she muttered with a sneer. Olivia didn't appreciate my need to mumble about Taylor aloud. Told off for mumbling, I went for normal-volume conversational tone, and even though Olivia looked like she wanted to murder me, I got to tell someone about my relationship woes. I was allowed five minutes a day on the topic after Olivia got over the fact that glaring at me didn't make me stop.

I sneered at Olivia who looked to be enjoying herself.

"I can't wait for you to meet her," Taylor said.

"Yeah. It should be awesome." I grimaced and Olivia cracked a rare smile as she pretended not to listen in.

"Is it going to be weird? You know, me introducing my gay best friend to my girlfriend?"

Hell, yes. It was going to be awful, awkward and in every way weird. "No weirder than me introducing you to my girlfriend, I guess."

"You're with someone?" Taylor practically gasped in my ear.

"What?"

"Is she coming with you?" Taylor's voice sounded odd. Like she was trying to be all light and disinterested.

"Who?"

"Your girlfriend."

I screwed up my face in confusion and shook my head. Taylor *was* sounding weird. Like maybe she was jealous. I gasped. Taylor Robbins sounded jealous of a girlfriend I didn't even have. *Lightbulb moment.* "I, ah, don't know." Maybe this was my angle. Maybe this was how I was going to finally make headway with Taylor. Going with the story, I said, "I think she has plans, so I'm waiting to hear back from her."

There was a lengthy silence before she asked, "It's Olivia, isn't it?"

"Olivia?" I looked up as the woman in question looked over at me with her head cocked.

"She's been domesticating you, with all those cooking lessons. Did you find a way to…thank her?" Taylor sounded quiet now.

"Taylor, my sex life is not open for discussion." I slapped my forehead when I replayed that. It sounded like an admission of sleeping with Olivia. Olivia, for her part, looked appalled. *Fair enough*, I thought.

Taylor gasped this time. "Oh, my God. You really did sleep with her. Didn't you?"

"No, I haven't slept with Olivia."

Olivia made a strangled noise in her throat. I looked at her in concern, wondering if she was about to vomit.

"So, she's not your girlfriend?"

I panicked. Taylor had shown some inclination of interest for the first time *ever*, I think, and no way in hell was I about to lose it. I turned around, tucked my chin into my chest and said as quietly as I could, "Yes, she's my…girlfriend, but no, we haven't…" I cleared my throat and blushed. "It's really none of your business." I peeked back to see if Olivia heard me. Affirmative. I averted my gaze from the lasers of Olivia's blue eyes boring into me. *I'm in trouble.* Olivia stood and closed the distance between us. *God, she was intimidating.* I added it to my list.

"So you invited her to come up?"

"I…yes?"

"So you're both coming tomorrow?"

"Yeah, straight after our anatomy exam."

"That's great. Umm…see you soon then?"

"Yep. See you soon."

"Love you."

"Yep," I said, quickly hanging up the call as Olivia reached for my phone.

"Are you mental!" Olivia screeched.

Cowering away, I shook my head. "She thought I was with someone and jumped to conclusions. I'm sorry, it was out of my control."

"How is telling her a complete lie out of your control. You just told her I was your girlfriend!"

"She was jealous," I said, standing and still finding myself looking up into her eyes. "She sounded hurt."

"Perhaps because you hadn't told her about your fake girlfriend yet. Ever think of that?"

All the wind left my sails. No, I didn't think of that angle at all. I shared everything with Taylor, so her suddenly thinking I had a girlfriend thanks to a few misunderstood words must have stung. I swore under my breath and sat down. No matter how hard I tried, there was still that flicker of hope in my chest that perhaps Taylor had been jealous, and not just hurt that her friend hadn't disclosed vital information. Mulling over that as Olivia paced in agitation around the apartment, I turned on my best puppy dog eyes and looked over at her.

She froze when she glanced at me. "No," she said abruptly. "Why?"

"What do you mean, *why*? In fact, I should be asking you that. *Why*, Darcy, do you think me pretending to be your girlfriend is going to help with your ridiculous infatuation with your best friend?"

"Because then she'll see how great I am as a partner. I'm perfect for her, but I never had the nerve to tell her how I felt."

"Perhaps that's exactly what you should be doing, confessing your feelings, not creating an elaborate ruse to force her into action."

"It'll help me see if she wants me. If she's jealous, then I know she feels something for me. Please. I'll do anything you want."

She narrowed her eyes. "I said no. I'm not going to parade myself around as if I'm attracted to you."

"Please?" I stood, my hands pressed together in a beg. "I'll stop watching TV. I'll stop singing under my breath. I'll throw out all my Reese pieces. *Anything.*"

"What part of *no* do you not understand?"

"I'll cook for the rest of the school year."

Olivia surprised us both with laughter. "How is that beneficial to me in any fashion?"

Offended, I propped my hands on my hips. "Hey, I can cook. I learned from the best."

She gave me a shrewd look and pointed her finger in my direction. "Sweet talking won't get you anywhere."

"I can cook the basics. Omelets. Salad. Chicken. Pasta. Think of all the time it'll save you. All that time you could spend studying instead." I added more incentive. "I'll do the laundry, in fact, I can do it as I work at Sunny's. There's another hour or two saved. I can, I can…" I looked around the apartment for more bribery material. "I'll be your slave."

Olivia sucked her bottom lip into her mouth ever-so-slightly, chewing on the inside of the flesh. That was her tell that she was thinking her options over.

"You will use the shower timer."

I deflated. I loved my long hot showers and detested having to be restricted to five minutes on non-hair-washing days, but I was desperate to see if my inkling was right. "Fine."

"You will stop your daily whining about Taylor."

I doubted that was possible, but I said, "Fine. Anything."

"Very well. On this *one* occasion, I will pretend to be your…girlfriend." She said the word like it was bitter on her tongue.

I groaned. At least no one would be surprised when we pretended to break up, too.

"You're paying for my ticket."

I grimaced at Olivia's departing form. *Damn.*

໙

After scrubbing the feel of Dolores off our hands, Olivia and I left the examination lab together.

"How did you think you did?" I asked her as the taxi took us to the airport, wondering if I had labeled the parts of my cadaver correctly.

"I'm sure I'll pass."

"Me too. I think I mixed up the connective tissue at the end, though." Time was running out, so I hastily labeled the anterior nerves and tendons of the wrist I had to inspect.

"Perhaps if you snacked less when studying, you'd have retained that information instead of wasting energy on metabolizing sugar."

"The Reese's? Yeah, maybe."

Olivia's gaze dropped to my hips and thighs. "Sugar not instantly utilized gets stored elsewhere."

"Yes, I know that. Why do you think I run? I have to maintain this figure somehow."

"You run so you can eat more rubbish. Your figure would maintain itself if you didn't ingest greasy foods every day of the week."

I couldn't argue with that.

Paying our cab driver and waiting silently in the terminal, we were soon airborne and headed for Duluth. Leveling out at thousands of feet above ground, I swore swiftly and rather loudly, earning the scorn of every mother and grandmother that could pinpoint me. Olivia covered her face, pretending she didn't know me. She did, however, whisper, "What is wrong with you?"

"I'm about to come out to my parents!" I said with a harsh urgent whisper. "Oh, God. Oh, God. I didn't think this through."

Olivia had the nerve to chuckle at that.

"Shut up," I muttered before wrapping my arms around my head and rocking back and forth like a crazed person.

Olivia stopped chuckling and stilled my movement with a hand on my shoulder. "If they love you, it will be okay."

"I know, and they do, and they'll be okay with this. I just wish…I've known how I've felt since I was thirteen. I should have told them before now."

Olivia patted my shoulder then quickly moved it away. "Wait. You've never had a girlfriend?"

I shook my head.

"So how exactly are you planning to convince this Taylor fool that you're the perfect person for her? What experience do you have being in a relationship with someone?"

I took a deep breath. Olivia was right. This was the dumbest plan ever. Maybe I should march in there and confess everything to Taylor. My mind took me away in a scenario full of sunshine and slow motion running, imagining the woman of my dreams crashing into my arms and sealing our feelings with a kiss. That would be so perfect. "You're right," I said, my head still hidden behind my hands. Emerging, I sighed. "I should tell her how I feel. Get my feelings out there and…" I shrugged. "Take a risk."

"You could have come to this conclusion before we left Boston."

"Sorry."

Olivia shook her head and pulled her textbook for Human Genetics from her backpack. Our ride in the plane, and on the bus was silent except for the occasional banter on the weather, seating arrangements, and some displeased words about my bag of donuts. I refused to share any with her after she scorned the existence of yellow icing.

∞

"Darcy!" My mother squealed when we arrived, gathering me in her arms. "My baby."

"Mom," I whined into her shoulder as she squeezed me tightly.

"And this must be your girlfriend?" she said, launching herself at Olivia and wrapping her in a fierce bear hug.

"Wait. You know about Olivia?"

"Of course, dear. I can read that subtext lingo stuff."

"Subtext lingo stuff?" I raised my eyebrows.

"Well, you see, honey, when you called, Olivia came up more and more. Your father and I have always known that the fairer sex was your preference, and so I assumed something was going on, but you were too worried to tell us."

My jaw hovered somewhere near the floor as my mother so casually informed me that, yes, she and dad knew I was gay, and by the way, we think you have a crush on your roommate.

"So, anyway, after Taylor came out with that darling woman, Charli, we finally figured it out."

I cautiously said, "What?"

"That you two must have experimented as teenagers. We asked her about it and she denied it, of course, but she mentioned Olivia and you two might be…you know…experimenting all on your own."

Olivia looked green.

I felt nauseous and woozy. I'm pretty sure coming out shouldn't happen in a very public bus terminal with a woman that could barely stand you pretending to be my girlfriend.

Messy.

"Right. Mom. Can we get home now?"

"Of course. I've got you both set up in your room."

"Oh, I don't think—"

"Nonsense," Mom cut Olivia off. "I'm no prude. Why, Darcy's father and I had quite the pre-marital affair."

I slapped my hand over my eyes. This was going from bad to worse.

"Come. Come," my mother called as she disappeared in the direction of the parking lot.

"I'm so sorry," I said, rounding on Olivia. "I should never have dragged you into this."

"No, you shouldn't have, but I shouldn't have let you bribe me into this either. I'm afraid that for now, we're stuck together."

I grimaced.

"Take my hand."

I stared at her for a heartbeat. "What?"

"My hand. Hold it."

"Seriously?"

With a frustrated noise, she snatched my hand and yanked me closer to her. "Come along, *sweetheart.*"

Chapter Four

Sleeping next to a woman was something I had experienced before. Taylor and I had many sleepovers as we grew up. Of course, now my mother probably imagined them as sordid experiments. Oh, how I wished that were the case.

Sleeping next to Olivia, however, was freaking me out. Since we left the bus station, she had held my hand, touched me casually on the arm and leg, and had smiled. Olivia didn't do smiling unless I'd done something particularly stupid, or she was doing that cruel evil grin thing. She was unnerving me with all this *nice*.

"Stop fidgeting, for God's sake," she snapped at me through the dark.

"Sorry, I can't help it."

"Pining for your childhood sweetheart again?"

"No, wondering if you're going to murder me in my sleep." There was a long pause. "God, you're not, are you?"

"It would certainly make my life easier."

"You'd have to get a new roommate," I said.

Another pause. "You have a point."

"Thank you."

"Now stay still and sleep."

"Yes, ma'am."

Grinning to myself in the dark, and feeling a lot calmer about Olivia's return to form, I let my dreams carry me to Neverland and beyond. My dreams were lovely. In them, a warm summer breeze wisped lazily through the morning air. It smelled fresh. Like vanilla. In the distance, I could see a woman in a summer dress silhouetted in the early light. She was facing away from me, hands to the side and capturing the breeze and the soft dandelion fuzz floating on the wind. I wrapped my hands around her, inhaling vanilla and jasmine. Smiling, I pressed my face into her neck and dropped open-mouthed kisses there. She sighed and tilted her head. I had never felt lighter, happier, or more in love.

Then an alarm tore me from my dream. Or it should have.

I woke to find the woman in my dreams still in my arms and smelling like vanilla. Fuzzy with sleep, I frowned. Blinking my eyes, I tried to focus, and then there was a sharp pinch on my hand.

"Ow!" I squealed and jumped away from the woman I was curled around, and more than freaked out because she was real.

"Serves you right for taking advantage of me," Olivia snapped as she hastily got out of bed.

"Olivia?" My eyes rushed wide open. "Oh, my God!" I had been wrapped around the woman, rather intimately, I realized as the cold morning air hit my legs. Legs that had been intertwined with hers. My arm had been wrapped around her waist before she pinched it. I looked at my hand to find a welt forming. "You pinched me."

"You groped me."

"I did not."

"You were kissing my neck!"

"Oh, God. Was I?"

Olivia began rummaging through her meticulously packed bag. "Where is the shower in this place? I feel the need to sanitize myself."

Dramatic as always. "Down the hall, first left. Hard to miss." My childhood home was tiny. Upstairs were two bedrooms, a bathroom, and a corner my mother used to worship all things sewing. Downstairs a renovated kitchen took up one entire side of the house and included the dining room. A lounge and entryway filled up the remainder of the space.

Olivia left the bedroom and I called out after her. "You'd be lucky to have me grope you."

She paused and I heard my mother giggling from somewhere in the hall. *Oops.*

Olivia turned, taking a moment to acknowledge the mother I couldn't see and smiled at me. It was weird. Then she said,

"Honey, you know how I feel about being intimate under your parents' roof." The way she said intimate should have been illegal. My skin buzzed and I began chastising myself for feeling a little turned on by it. Olivia Boyd came with a great big yellow and black hazard sign. I wanted nothing to do with it, and I was tempting fate enough by asking her to pretend to like me. Actually getting her to like me, or for me to like her, was a recipe for disaster.

"The bitchy black widow would eat me alive," I muttered to myself as I climbed out of bed when I was left alone.

"Pardon, dear?"

"Mom? I…nothing. Good morning."

"Morning. How'd you sleep?" She looked at the rumpled sheets of my twin bed. Yet another point of complaint from Olivia when she spotted it last night.

"No. No way. You're on the floor. I'm not sharing the space the size of a shoebox with you," she had said.

Tired and spun out, I didn't bother arguing and climbed in beside her anyway.

To mom, I said, "Ah…I slept really well, actually."

"And Olivia?"

I shrugged. "She seemed peaceful enough." Right up to the moment I began kissing her neck. Suddenly my lips tingled and the sensation of them touching warm scented skin came to mind. I withheld a groan and firmly reminded myself that I disliked Olivia Boyd with passionate intent.

"Oh, good," said Mom. "Come downstairs when you're done. We've lots to do today."

∞

The 'lots to do' was an understatement. We shifted the dining space around to fit eight people. Taylor's parents usually joined our family, but with our *girlfriends* visiting, we had to locate two more chairs and rearrange some of the furniture. The turkey had been put in the oven at daybreak, Mom and Olivia were attending to the vegetables requiring roasting, and I was stirring the cranberry sauce Mom had put together. It was my job to stand by the stove and monitor it. Olivia and Mom eyed me warily to make sure I didn't ruin it.

"What! I can cook," I snapped at them when I was once again assessed in my ability.

"Omelets. You can cook omelets," Olivia said.

"And that other stuff you showed me. And besides, I make a mean omelet. I distinctly remember you groaning with pleasure last time." Olivia smirked over the potatoes she was dusting with flour while Mom hid a knowing grin. I narrowed my eyes at the pair of them. "The point is," I said, stomping my foot. "I am more than capable of looking after this jam thing."

"Cranberry sauce, dear." Mom looked at the stove. "And it's burning."

"What?" I whipped around to find it bubbling wildly. Stirring it quickly, I was dismayed to find the bottom was stuck to the pot. "Damn it."

"It's okay, honey. I'll make some more. Perhaps you could go help your father."

"He's watching TV."

"Exactly, dear. Olivia and I have got this."

"But…" I blew out a dismayed breath of air. "Fine." I walked out the kitchen and found my dad in the adjacent room. "Hey," I said as I flopped onto the couch.

"Hey." He gave me a sidelong glance. "You okay there, sweetie?"

"I'm fine. Who's playing today?"

"Lions and Giants, Cowboys and Eagles, and Ravens and Steelers."

Dad and I always went for the Lions and Cowboys on Thanksgiving. The third game preference was usually given to the team we disliked least. "Go Ravens then?"

Dad nodded. "Ravens it is."

I heaved out a sigh and watched some of the pre-game show for the Lions and Giants game.

"What's cooking?" he asked in his roundabout way of asking what was wrong.

"I got kicked out, so why don't you go ask the head chef and her new favorite sous chef."

"Sous chef?"

"Second in charge."

"Oh, right." Dad sipped at his cup of tea. "She seems really nice."

"Olivia?" At dad's nod, I nodded in reply. "Yeah, she is." I hoped my nose didn't grow.

"She a doctor, too?"

"Yeah, we're both doing pre-med."

Dad nodded again. He was a mechanic working at the mines outside of Virginia, and my mother taught elementary school in Aurora. They had no expectations of me beyond finding steady work. My wish to become a doctor since I was seven stuck with me, though, and they did everything they could to make that a reality. I owed them more than I could ever repay.

"So, the Mustang needs some lovin'. Let's go play?"

I grinned. It would be cold out in the back shed, but my baby had been neglected for months. "Did the manifold arrive?"

"Yep. Got the head re-bored and found some gaskets off old Tom. He brought them into the shop last week."

I smiled at dad and we rugged up in scarfs, gloves and winter coats. Being just south of the Canadian border, late November was chilly at best. The lake down the back gave us a small advantage in temperature. I glanced down the path that led to dad's private pier and boathouse. They had done well buying this two-acre property back before living on the edge of civilization was popular. They'd been here, nestled between the lake, mountain, and ski resort for four decades.

Dad caught my attention as he heaved at the large rolling door hiding my baby.

I quickly pulled off the dust cover and ran my hands over my pride and joy, rusty as she was. Soon, dad and I had the hood open and our arms greasy up to our elbows as we reassembled the manifold and replaced the head.

"Oh!" Olivia's voice interrupted us some time later. She stared at me and my greasy arms as I looked up. "You're filthy."

I grinned.

"Please tell me you don't plan to be a surgeon?"

I shook my head as it occurred to me I had no idea what Olivia planned to specialize in either. "I wasn't planning to be."

"Good. Because you'll ruin your hands with this sort of labor." She peered under the hood of my car. "What are you two doing?"

"Making my baby purr."

"Excuse me?"

Dad chuckled. "I gather she hasn't introduced you to Mavis yet?"

"Mavis?"

I walked over to Olivia, who flinched away from me as though greasiness could leap across a two-foot gap. "This," I said with a proud sweep of my hand. "Is Mavis. My first car. My baby."

"It's…" Olivia frowned at it. "Rusty."

"We're doing the paint job last. Dad's a mechanic, and he's been helping me restore her."

"*It*."

"Pardon?"

"It's a car, it can't have a gender."

"Sorry, but *Mavis* is most definitely a she. Like another woman I know, she's temperamental, she bites, and it takes a lot of hard work to make her happy."

Olivia gave me a suspicious glare. "I hope you didn't just compare me to your car."

Dad chuckled again, the sound drowned out slightly by the wrench he was working with.

I shrugged. "She has her quirks, but with time and patience, I'm slowly working them out." That definitely held true for both my car and Olivia. Staring at the hunk of metal in front of me,

I said without thinking, "Mavis is beautiful, and one day, she's going to purr for me." Smiling, I looked to Olivia to see if she heard me and frowned at the shocked expression on her face. My words echoed back to me and I gasped. "No, I didn't...umm..." I looked over to my dad. I leaned forward and whispered. "I wasn't trying to...umm..."

"To what? Hit on me with a cheesy line?"

"I wasn't hitting on you," I whispered back.

"Thank God for that."

About to retort with a line about how she'd be lucky to have me hit on her, Taylor came screeching into the shed. "Darcy!" she cried and launched herself into my arms. Laughing and squeezing her back as much as I could without imparting grease on her clothes. I said my hello's into the hair that had covered my face. She pulled back slightly and planted a kiss on my lips. Just like old times.

Olivia cleared her throat as we smiled at each other. I quickly stepped back, reluctant to let her out of my arms. "Oh. Taylor, this is Olivia. Olivia...Taylor."

"Hi," Taylor said, holding out her hand. Olivia looked at it before tentatively shaking it and inclined her head in greeting. "You're beautiful," Taylor added.

Jealousy tickled my chest. *Why couldn't she say things like that to me?*

"Thank you," Olivia said. "You're not as repulsive as I had imagined either."

Taylor gasped. "What?"

Olivia smiled, diffusing the situation with an action that lit up her eyes. "I'm kidding."

Taylor laughed dutifully and seemed happy. "Everyone's up at the house. Are you going to clean up and join us?" she asked me, looking at the grease.

I nodded. "I'll be right up."

"Great, I can't wait for you to meet Charli."

I smiled, but my heart twisted and I'm pretty sure my eyes looked lifeless. "Great."

Taylor moved off towards the house, leaving me alone with Olivia. "Not repulsive?" I whispered to her.

Olivia shrugged and we both noticed Taylor stop to wait for her. "Coming?"

Olivia nodded and leaned in, making me my brace myself. She planted a kiss on my cheek and whispered, "You have grease on your nose. Cute."

"I...okay."

Blinking, I watched her go, unable to help myself from looking over the jeans she wore, and only noticing Taylor's curious glare when Olivia turned and caught me staring. I smiled stiffly and quickly turned around with a clearing of my throat.

"You've got it bad," Dad said.

"Bad?"

"You compared your girlfriend to your car. Your pride and joy. The only thing that you've been in love with...ever."

"I didn't mean to."

"Oh, honey, I think you did. Going to make her purr, huh?"

God. Death by embarrassment. "Shut up," I mumbled and began helping him clean up. Tools away, shed closed, and trying not to touch my jacket with my scrubbed, but still greasy, hands. I ran up to the house through the chilly air and barreled through the back door.

Someone screamed as I hit them with the swinging wood.

"Sorry!" I yelled quickly, to find I'd hit a stranger. She was now covered in whatever beverage she had been drinking. "Oh, geez. I'm so sorry," I said, reaching out to try and sweep the drink away from her clothes. Of course, the grease on my hands made the mess worse. I swore.

"Darcy!"

"Sorry," I said to Mom and then again to the woman I assumed was Charli. "I'm so sorry."

"What is wrong with you," Taylor said, sidling in beside her girlfriend. "You just ruined her blouse."

I balked a little, unused to hearing Taylor's annoyed voice directed at me. "I said I was sorry, okay? How was I supposed to know someone was hiding out behind the door?"

Charli put a hand on Taylor's arm. "It's okay."

"You sure?" Taylor asked.

Charli nodded. "You must be Darcy?" she said to me. "It's lovely to finally meet the woman my girlfriend won't shut up about."

I gaped a little. What was that supposed to mean? Taylor talked about me a lot? I looked at her to find her blushing. "Umm…hi," I said to Charli. Despite knowing what this woman's hair and eye color were, I didn't know much beyond the fact she was managing Taylor's store. Charli was gorgeous. With bronze skin, her eyes were like chocolate and she was very curvy. *Very.* I could see why Taylor was attracted to her. I didn't stand a chance. "I, uh…better go clean up." With a tight smile, I pushed between the couple and gave Olivia a glance on my way out of the kitchen. She was frowning at me. Probably deciding my manners were appalling, I'd guess.

Clean, grease-free and clothed in something that wasn't a decade old, I made my way back downstairs. Charli and Taylor were curled up on the couch together watching the pre-game show and looking very cozy. Charli's arm was around Taylor's shoulders, and after spotting me walking in, Taylor cuddled against her further. I had to look away. Seeing her nuzzling against someone that could have been me was heartbreaking.

A hand slipped around my waist and I yelped a little.

"Boo," Olivia said, chuckling silently to herself at my reaction.

A glance told me Taylor had looked our way, and wanting to capitalize on the opportunity and see if my inkling was correct, I leaned up and kissed Olivia on the cheek as I wrapped my arm around her. "Hi," I whispered, trying to sound sultry and alluring. I missed the mark spectacularly and Olivia raised an eyebrow at me in amusement.

"Hi," she said, purring into my ear and showing me exactly how it was done. I shivered and leaned into her. Remembering suddenly that I started this to see what Taylor would do, I looked back to the sofa. She wasn't looking at me, but she'd pulled away from Charli and looked stiff.

I had no idea what that meant. *Was she jealous? Had Charli annoyed her? Did she have cramps?*

"Dinner will be ready in twenty, everyone," Mom called from the kitchen. I barely listened as I tried to plan my next move.

Tugging at Olivia's waist, I took her to the relative privacy of the upstairs landing.

"I want you to kiss me," I whispered to her questioning glare at being led around like a dog.

Her eyebrows shot up. "Kiss you?"

I nodded. "I can't quite tell if Taylor is interested."

"Trust me, she is."

My eyes lit up. "Really?"

"She was interrogating me when we came back inside, and then practically wrapped herself all over her girlfriend a little too enthusiastically."

I bit my lip in thought. "I don't know if that means she wants me, though. She could just be doing the best friend interrogation thing."

Olivia shrugged.

"Maybe…" I said, rubbing my chin in thought. "Maybe, if she saw us kissing, then I'll try to get her alone and see what she thinks of it."

Olivia sighed. "I don't recall agreeing to any sort of affectionate touching, let alone kissing."

"Hey, you're the one that held my hand first, and you kissed me on the cheek. I never asked you to do that."

"I was trying to sell the relationship for you. You should be thanking me."

"What do you want from me in order for you to kiss me?"

"I want you to sleep on the floor tonight."

That was going to be horrible. "Okay," I said, nodding in quick agreement. "Let's practice," I said, leaning up to kiss her.

"Wait. Now?"

"She can't very well see our first kiss. It's going to be awkward. Let's get it out of the way."

Huffing, Olivia said, "Fine. Let's get this over with."

Smiling, I leaned in and did what I'd witnessed in the movies. I tilted my head, stuck out my tongue and opened and shut my mouth. Olivia pulled away with a yelp.

"What the heck was that?"

"A kiss."

Olivia burst out laughing. "That was more like a dying fish gasping for air than a kiss."

I stepped back and crossed my arms to pout at her. "Yeah, well, maybe we're just not compatible. It's hardly a surprise."

Olivia settled into chuckling and shook her head. "No one would be compatible with that." Cocking her head, she studied me for a moment. "Have you ever kissed anyone before? Apart from my neck?"

I sniffed and looked down the stairs. "No."

"And you're how old?"

"Twenty-three."

"How is it you've never kissed anyone?"

"I'm gay, remember. With a crush on my straight best friend. I didn't want to kiss anyone but her, no matter how many spin-the-bottle games Taylor tried to make me play with the guys from school."

Olivia raised her hands in surrender. "Hey, I didn't mean to judge."

"You always mean to judge."

Olivia huffed. "Not this time."

"Yeah, well, it hardly matters anyway. I'll strike the kissing thing off. Maybe we can snuggle or something instead."

"Or maybe, I can teach you how to kiss."

I eyed her warily.

"Consider it a public service. If you ever do get together with Taylor, trust me, you're going to want to know what to do."

I unhooked my arms from my chest and rolled my shoulders. "Okay."

"Good." Olivia stepped over to me, involuntarily forcing me to step backward against the wall. She smirked and stepped flush against me. "Give me your hand." I held one up, and she placed it on her cheek, resting my thumb against her lips. They were seriously soft.

I licked my own.

"Now…kissing is soft and gentle. At least to start with. Usually. Sometimes it's rough and needy."

"That's confusing."

She smiled. "It depends on the situation. For Taylor, you'll need to go slow and tender. Like this." My thumb that had been resting against her lips as she spoke became the center of attention. Opening her lips slightly, she placed gentle kisses against the pad.

I swallowed thickly. As much as I hated to admit it, this was kind of turning me on.

She opened her eyes and looked into mine. "Understand?"

I nodded.

"When you're ready, you tentatively explore with your tongue." She kissed my thumb again, this time, however, she let her tongue slide out and skim across my thumb.

God damn!

"Have you got it?" she asked, ceasing her kisses and opening her eyes again.

I nodded and licked my lips again.

"Show me."

Swallowing hard, I took a deep breath and leaned forward, closing the six-inch gap between us. I did like she showed me and carefully took her bottom lip between mine in a soft kiss. I repeated the action, moving my lips in time with hers. Ready to try the tongue thing, I let it slide out on my next kiss and embarrassed myself with an involuntary moan. She didn't seem to mind, because the next thing I knew, I was being pushed against the wall as she began to stroke my mouth with her tongue. My graduation from soft and tender to rough and needy escalated as I followed her lead and my instincts and set myself free in my first ever kiss.

It wasn't until we heard a gasp that we broke apart. Discovering I'd grasped Olivia's backside with one hand while tangling the other in her dark locks, I quickly let go, expecting Olivia to fly off me in offense. She didn't move. Leaving her hands where they were, she tilted her head slightly and we both saw Taylor at the top of the stairs staring at us intently.

"It wasn't me!" I blurted out. *God, why did I say that?* Blushing from head to toe, I blamed the surge of lust that had traveled my body forcing random neurons to fire in my brain.

Taylor, predictably, looked at me oddly.

Clearing my throat, I said, "Never mind."

"Oh…okay. Umm, sorry for interrupting. Carry on." She ran back downstairs.

Only when she was out of sight, that Olivia let go of my neck and waist. *Wait, was her hand under my top?* Clearing her throat, she said, "I think it's safe to say that worked."

I nodded. "That's…" I cleared my husky throat. "That's good. Umm…thanks."

"You're welcome."

Straightening out our clothes, we awkwardly started to descend the stairs. "So, umm…" I said before we reached the bottom. "Did I pass?" I asked, referring to my kissing lesson.

Olivia stopped and looked at me. "I believe you did."

"Great."

Olivia gave me a tight-lipped smile and headed for the dining room. I watched her go and was pretty sure I had fallen a little in lust with her. *Damn she could kiss.*

Chapter Five

Lunch was a conglomeration of noise, over-consumption of food, and football updates. Charli, I soon discovered, was kind of nice. The fact she had tea and grease on her shirt took the edge off my jealousy at any rate. Taylor and I chatted as we always do, but from time to time, I found her staring at me. I smiled at her each time and we continued eating or conversing.

Dessert was being served, Taylor's mother's famous pumpkin pie, and that was when Olivia rested her hand on my upper thigh, making me jerk and bump the table.

"Pass the cream, please," she whispered into my ear.

"O-okay." I did as requested and she gave my thigh a squeeze. Looking over at Taylor, I saw her scowling as she stabbed at her pie. Olivia was a genius. Dropping my hand below the table, I rested it over Olivia's and squeezed. Our fingers intertwined, and that's how we remained for the rest of the meal and post-dinner beverages.

"You guys really do make sweet couples," my mother said as dinner wound up, looking to Olivia and I and then Taylor and Charli.

Taylor smiled and wrapped her arm around Charli's. "Thank you."

I smiled at Mom.

"How did you two meet?" Charli asked me and Olivia. I gave her a look of surprise.

"Taylor didn't tell you?"

Charli shrugged. "All I know is that you're living in Boston doing med school and living with a nightmare." She looked at Taylor. "What was it you call her? Dr. Crazy?"

I felt Olivia's hand clench mine. Her fierce grip was crushing the bones in my hand. I tried not to scream in pain.

At least Taylor looked contrite when she whispered to Charli, "Ah, honey that was Olivia."

"Olivia is the nightmare roommate?"

I bowed my head and stifled a groan.

"Yes, I am," Olivia spoke up and relaxed her grip. "Darcy has the manners and behavior of a teenager on summer break. Domestication has been difficult for her."

"Hey!" I said, looking up at Olivia. Her eyes were twinkling. She was having fun. I glared and she smiled.

"Am I right, sweetheart?" she asked me.

"I guess," I said with a mumble.

"She taught her how to cook. Anyone that can achieve that feat with my daughter is a keeper in my book," Mom said proudly.

"I taught her how to do her makeup," Taylor said softly from the other side of the table.

"She cleans as well," Olivia said directly at Taylor, obviously hearing her muttered words.

"That's it! You're staying," Mom said with a laugh. "Imagine that, *two* doctors in the family."

"She only wanted to become a doctor because of me," Taylor said glumly, earning a frown from her girlfriend.

Mom beamed at her. "Yes, she did, dear. I can't thank you enough for it. I haven't seen Darcy so happy."

"Happy? All they do is bicker."

Mom smiled and nodded merrily. "Exactly."

The table was silent for a moment as that was digested along with the dessert.

"Well, as…lovely as this conversation is, I need to walk off my pie," I said, choosing the fastest route to escape.

"Me too," Taylor said, standing up abruptly. "We need to catch up."

"Yeah."

"Bring in some more wood when you come back," Dad said. "The old stuff at the back of the pile please."

"Sure," I said. Releasing Olivia's hand, I gave her an awkward smile. "Here goes nothing," I whispered.

She didn't answer and instead, looked away from me.

That was awkward.

"I'll be back soon to help clean up," I called out to Mom on my way out. A few seconds later, I was alone with Taylor. Finally.

"Down the lake?" she asked, referring to a track that wound around the water.

"Yeah. Sounds good."

Walking silently, we reached the water and began our trek to the northwest.

"I can't believe you have a girlfriend," Taylor said, breaking the silence that had kept us company for ten minutes.

"I can't believe *you* have one."

"You never told me you were a lesbian. I had to figure it out. Why?"

I stopped. "I didn't know what you'd say. Your friendship was more important."

Taylor smiled and took my hands in hers. "It's because of that I would have understood. I don't care what you are, you're my best friend and I love you."

I smiled thinly. "I love you."

She let out a long breath and stared at me. "Do you?"

Here it was. Here was the perfect moment. "I do."

"In what way?"

"I…" I sighed and looked down at my hands through the steam coming from my mouth. "I don't know how to say it."

"You should have said something, Darce."

"I never knew how. You had Jack, and…well…the other guys. Besides, you were straight. I didn't want you to think I was coming on to you all the time or anything. It would have been weird."

Taylor remained silent for a while. "How did you know?"

"Know what?"

"That you were into girls?"

I shrugged. "I guess I just noticed them more. Guys never did anything for me."

"Did you have a crush on anyone?"

Yeah, you. "Not really."

"What about Nancy. She was pretty."

She also wasn't Taylor. "I suppose."

We continued walking and Taylor said, "I'm not straight anymore. I'm bi."

That confession made me think of Olivia.

Taylor looked down to our feet and sighed. "When Charli arrived, she reminded me so much of you."

"So you decided to fall for her?"

Taylor bit her lip. "I guess." She looked back into my eyes. "But she's not you."

I nearly fainted. "Me?"

"I have a confession. When I found out about Olivia, I was…" She rubbed her neck. "I felt jealous."

"You did?"

Taylor nodded and stepped closer as her hand reached up to caress my cheek. I was suddenly very thankful to Olivia for teaching me how to kiss. Taylor's lips were just there and if I was bold enough, I could leap across and kiss her. I recalled my lesson. Soft lips, gentle tongue, and then all that heady urgency that had Olivia's hand snaking up my top. I blinked and quickly straightened up. Olivia was my girlfriend, pretend as she was, but Taylor had a legitimate one. It was one thing to try and find out if Taylor was interested in me, it was another to be the other woman.

"What is it?" Taylor asked me.

"Olivia."

"Olivia?"

"Umm, she'll be expecting me back soon."

"Mmm," Taylor said, sounding a little annoyed. "Is she one of those clingy, controlling types?"

"Controlling, yes. Clingy, no."

Taylor and I headed back toward the house. "She's not the kind of girl I expected you to fall for, you know?"

"Oh?" I said, keen to hear more. "And what's my type?"

"Someone fun, carefree, relaxed. Someone you have things in common with, like NFL teams."

I smiled. "Olivia is a Packers fan."

"Figures."

I shrugged. "I like it. It gives me something to rile her up about."

"Except the Packers beat us last time."

I pouted. "Yeah."

"My point is, how did she win you over? She's…" Taylor stopped and faced me. "Not like me."

"You?" I said, hearing the gasp in my voice.

"Yeah. I'm fun. I know all your secrets."

"But…Charli?"

Taylor averted her eyes. "She's…really great."

A knife twisted in my chest. Of course she was great.

"But, she's not you either."

"What?"

Taylor rubbed a hand through her blonde up-do. "Ugh."

"Taylor, what are you saying?" *And why did I sound desperate?*

"I'm saying that I miss you, that's all. We've been inseparable since pre-school and now…" She waved her hand with a sudden heated flourish toward the house. "Now all I hear is Olivia this and Olivia that. You didn't even tell me you were dating her. That's something best friends do, Darcy."

She was right and I felt suitably chagrined. About to apologize, Taylor said, "She's no good for you."

"What?" I said in a half-whisper.

"She's a bully, Darce."

"She is not."

"Really? Then why did she throw out your food?" she asked, referring to the incident with the pizza.

"Because she wants me to eat healthier."

"And you can't watch TV."

"I don't have time to do that anyway."

Taylor looked flustered and her eyes seem to search for more ammunition. "She's stuck up, controlling, and she's all over you."

"What?" I swayed back a little taking in this new side of Taylor. Jealous as she clearly was, it didn't suit her. Something about her behavior made me step in and defend Olivia. Using my finger as my stand-in knightly sword, I pointed it at her. "Olivia is dedicated *not* controlling or stuck up. She's focused, and she's going to be a brilliant doctor." I let my hand fall back to my side. "I didn't tell you about her because..." *It was a giant lie*, I filled in silently. "Because I've never done this before." *True*. I can say with certainty I've never bribed someone into dating me before. "I've never had feelings like this before." *Another truth*. Olivia made me marginally homicidal with some of her rules. "But I like her. I respect her, and she's important to me." I shocked myself to find my nose didn't feel like growing. I genuinely *did* feel those things for her. I think the kiss helped somewhat, because *damn*. I cleared my throat as my mind veered. "I'm sorry."

Taylor looked subdued. "I'm sorry, too. Friends?"

"Always."

We embraced, and as my arms wrapped around her, my brain couldn't help but supply useless information about how different she felt from Olivia. I caught the scent of Taylor's musky perfume, and for the first time in my life, I didn't shut my eyes and savor the smell.

∞

Heaving in a load of wood a few minutes later, Taylor and Charli, along with Taylor's parents, left, leaving the four of us to watch the football game. Unable to get my head into the action after my conversation with Taylor, I sat and stared at the screen blankly. I caught a few odd looks as I sighed loudly...again.

"Walk with me?" Olivia asked, taking my hand.

I nodded. Anything was better than sitting there replaying the moment I rejected Taylor Robbins.

"What's wrong with you?" Olivia asked the moment we reached the lake. Taking a similar path as Taylor and I, I shrugged in reply. "You've been a delightful example of a depressed human being since you returned from the lake with your secret lover. What happened?"

"I had a chance to kiss her." Olivia's hand tightened in mine. I looked down at the entwined fingers curiously. *Why was I still holding her hand?* "I didn't go through with it."

"What? Why? I thought that was the whole point of this ordeal?"

"It's one thing to find out if she's into me that way, it's entirely another to cheat on someone."

"You didn't kiss her because of Charli?"

"I didn't kiss her because of *you* and Charli."

"Me? What do I have to do with this?"

"You're my girlfriend…at least to Taylor you are. I'm hardly setting a good example by cheating on my first girlfriend to the first interested party, now am I?"

Olivia stared at me for a moment. "That is actually quite…noble of you. Who would've thought?"

I rolled my eyes. "I'm hardly without morals."

"Perhaps, however, I'm here in the capacity as a pretend girlfriend to stir some kind of jealousy in your best friend who also happens to be in a relationship."

I groaned. She had a point.

"Maybe we should break up?" she said.

"Why?"

"It might prompt her to part ways with Charli. Win-win."

A hollow victory. I sighed. "Maybe. Right now, I just want to walk."

Olivia nodded, and hand in hand we continued around to the far side of the lake. There, I led her down the Petersen's pier and we sat on the edge, dangling our feet over the water. Hands finally disengaged, I took comfort in the way her thigh pressed against mine on the narrow dock. I could smell the pine mixed with smoke in the crisp air, and across the gently rippling lake, I saw my childhood house standing solid and timeless.

"So, why medicine?" I asked, breaking the comfortable silence keeping us company.

Olivia took a long breath. "The human body has always fascinated me. I excelled in the sciences at school, and was advised by my career advisor to put my passion to good use."

"Where'd you go to school?"

Olivia glanced at me. "What is this? Twenty questions."

I shrugged. "Why not. I barely know you."

She huffed. "You first. Why medicine?"

"Taylor." Olivia frowned in confusion so I enlightened her. "We were seven and climbing trees near the house. She fell and cut herself badly when she caught the shed roof on the way down. I remember seeing the inside of her leg the gash was so deep. Blood everywhere." Olivia gasped. Rightfully so. It was a horrific wound. "Figuring that wasn't good, I shoved my hand hard down on her leg and screamed out for Mom." I fiddled with the wooden pole beside my leg, feeling the splintered wood. "I had my hand on her leg as we were rushed to the hospital. The doctor said I saved her life. I guess from then on, I knew that that's what I wanted to do...save lives."

Olivia reached for my hand and gave it a squeeze.

"So," I said after holding hands quietly for a few minutes as I lost myself in thoughts of my childhood friend covered in blood. "Where did you go to school?"

"The Bronx."

"You're a native New Yorker?"

Olivia shook her head. "Where did you go to school?"

"Aurora. You're not from New York?"

Olivia shook her head again. "I was born in Buffalo. I think."

"You think?"

She ignored me. "What are you going to specialize in?"

I shrugged. "I haven't really thought about it. I was going to walk out with a general practitioner license, but I think I'll wait until we're in clinical rotations to make up my mind."

"You *think* you were born in Buffalo?"

Olivia's gaze held fast on the water. "I was found on the doorstep of a convent."

"What?" I heard about stories like that in the news but had never really thought about what happened to those babies as they grew. I wondered if this is why Olivia was so defensive and determined to prove herself. I gave her hand a gentle squeeze. "And then what?"

"I believe it's my turn to ask a question." After a pause, she said, "Why Taylor?"

"Why am I in love with her?"

Olivia nodded.

I blew out a long breath. "I don't know. Lots of little things, I suppose. I began to notice other girls around me when I was thirteen. They were all into boys, but I found nothing special to get worked up over. Taylor really umm..." I held a hand out in front of my chest. "*Grew*, and I found I had a crush on her instead of the popular boy like the rest of them. She's the closest friend I've ever had and, I don't know, I love everything about her. Her smile. Her laugh. Her phobia of cockroaches." I chuckled to myself. "She was just...everything." I startled myself a little when it occurred to me that I said 'was.'

"What does she do?"

"Huh?" I blinked. "Uh, uh. My turn. Have you ever been in love?"

"Yes. Now, what does she do?"

"No, wait. More details please."

"You didn't specify for any. Answer my question."

"Taylor works at her dad's grocery store." I could see by the look on Olivia's face that she didn't approve. "She has an MBA from Minnesota U and is being trained to take over the business." That information didn't impress her either. "Tell me about your first love."

"That's not a question, it's a demand."

"Amuse me."

She huffed. "It was a guy I met when I was seventeen. We fell in love and fell out of it quite abruptly a year later."

"Why thanks, Mark Twain."

"What?"

"Your storytelling is woeful. There was no detail in that. Try again."

"Why should I?"

"Because I spilled my heart out to you."

"Which was entirely your choice."

"You asked me 'why Taylor,' it makes sense to elaborate. So, why this mystery seventeen-year-old?"

"It's my turn."

I rolled my eyes and groaned. "Fine. What do you want to know?"

"Once you've finished your MD, where are you going to go?"

"Here. I planned to come home and find work in Aurora or something. Somewhere close."

She looked confused by this. "What on earth for? You'll have an MD. You could go anywhere."

"This is my home. That's why. I love northern Minnesota. I love being close to my parents, and…well…Taylor is here."

"You're talented. Intelligent. If you were serious about saving people, then you should apply your skills elsewhere."

"Or…I may totally suck at clinical rotations and be nothing more than a GP."

"I find that hard to believe."

"Why, Miss Boyd, was that a compliment? Actually, several compliments." She scoffed and I smiled. "You think I'm talented?"

"You're not completely incompetent."

"You think I'm intelligent?"

"You have your moments."

I grinned broadly. "You like me, don't you?"

"Don't be absurd. I tolerate you, is all."

"Mmm hmm."

She clucked her tongue and avoided my eyes. Her hand, however, was still linked with mine. Something that fascinated me as I looked down at them. *How had we become so comfortable with each other to be able to hold hands for an hour?* I smiled. I wasn't going to complain. Olivia was an attractive woman, even if she was a pain in the ass.

"So what do you want to be when you grow up?" I asked her after shifting my attention away from wayward thoughts of attractive pre-med students.

My question obviously caught her by surprise, and she started to laugh. My face broke into a wide smile at the sound of it. "You should do that more often?"

"What?"

"Laugh."

"I laugh!" she said, immediately frowning.

"No, you chuckle derisively. Mostly you sneer."

"I do not!" She glared at me while I laughed quietly to myself. "Pediatrics."

"Huh?"

"I want to work in pediatrics."

"Oh. Really?"

"Why, don't you think I'm capable?"

"No...I just expected you to shoot for the stars, you know? Be a surgeon."

She sniffed and looked across the lake. "That's my second choice."

"Why pediatrics?"

Olivia took a deep breath and rushed it out. "Kids don't deserve to be in pain." She lowered her head to stare at our interlocked hands, and her hair fell across her face, obstructing my view. The mood shifted when she said quietly, "I want to help them."

Frowning with concern, I rubbed my thumb against the back of her hand. "Then you will," I whispered.

She nodded slightly to acknowledge my words, then a moment later, she cleared her throat and stood up so rapidly, I was tugged along for the ride and nearly fell into the water. Squealing with imminent doom, I latched on to her tightly. She obviously noticed the urgency and pulled me from my overbalanced view of the water below me and we ended up in a bear hug.

"Holy crap," I blurted as my heart tried to stop racing.

"Oops," she muttered, but then her shoulders started shaking.

"You better not be laughing," I said as I pulled back from her slightly to see her bite her lip…hard. She shook her head, but the tears shining in her eyes said a different story. "You *are* laughing! You nearly gave me hypothermia, and now you're amused? Some doctor you're going to make."

She kept laughing, her face going red with the effort of keeping it in. I couldn't help it. She was amazing to watch and I began to smile and shake my own shoulders with laughter. The dam released and she let her head fall onto my shoulder as the sound of her laughing echoed around the lake. As I laughed and shook my head at her, I added eccentric to my list of adjectives. Eccentric and sweet…in a not completely unattractive way.

Chapter Six

I drew random squiggles on my notepad as I procrastinated the research required to do my social medicine paper. The soft tones of Norah Jones filled my ears, as recommended by Olivia, and I zoned out to her sound. My mind was in northeast Minnesota. Taylor had messaged me incessantly since I left, wanting to know how I was, telling me how much she missed me and always adding a question about how Olivia was doing. My replies felt like I was going behind Olivia's back in some kind of screwed-up affair. It was insane. A few minutes ago, Taylor had sent me a countdown to Christmas. It was two weeks away.

I jerked with pain as the ear plugs were ripped from my ears.

"I said, are you listening to me?"

Rubbing my ears, I snarled at Olivia. "That hurts."

"Can you please clean the bathroom?"

"What?"

"You promised me you'd do it weekly, and by my count, it's been ten days."

"What are you doing for Christmas?"

Olivia looked slightly winded by that and her hands fell from her hips where she had propped them intimidatingly. "Pardon?"

"Christmas. Do you have plans?" My parents had bought me a ticket back in July, fully intending their only child to be home a Christmas, which was a blessing, because after the impromptu trip northwest for two, I had no money left.

She blinked my question. "I don't see what that has to do with the state of our bathroom."

"It has nothing to do with it. Besides, this is more important."

"I disagree. Showering without a colony of mold growing in the corner is. Please clean the bathroom. We can discuss empty holiday traditions afterward."

"Christmas isn't empty. It's all about giving and warmth and family and—" I nearly bit off my tongue when I realized what I was saying. "Oh."

Giving me a tight grimace, Olivia said, "Bathroom. Now. I'd like to shower today."

I nodded quickly and scrubbed away my insensitivity with bleach and a plastic bristle brush. "Idiot," I whispered as I rinsed the bleach away to reveal a sparkling shower stall. Mulling over ways to apologize to an orphan about how Christmas is awesome because it's about family, I suddenly frowned. Even babies given away by their parents could still enjoy Christmas. Right? Damn, maybe she was against it for religious reasons, or simply acting like Scrooge McDuck again. I ripped my gloves off and marched to the living area.

"What do you have against Christmas?" Olivia looked up at me, startled by my sudden appearance. "I don't buy the poor me routine. Surely orphans get Christmas, too."

She knitted her eyebrows together and stood from her chair. Damn, she was tall. "You think I'm looking for pity for simply detesting a religiously significant day because it's become all about profit margins and how much people can spend on their children?"

"That's not what it's like for me. It's always been about thanks and love."

"Yes, but for the majority, it's about the latest gadgets and games. I stopped believing in Santa Claus when I was five. And don't you dare bring up my heritage again. I'm not an orphan, I was abandoned by living, breathing parents, not by deceased ones. Christmas reminds me of the day I was left, practically frozen to death, on a cement doorstep."

I couldn't hide my shock and gasped loudly. "You were found on Christmas Day?"

She flinched and I suspect she hadn't meant to reveal that.

"You were born on Christmas?"

She ignored my question. "My *point* is, I'm not big into Christmas. And why are we even having this conversation?" She shook her head and stalked off to the kitchen.

"I wanted to see if you'd come home with me."

"For Christmas?"

"No, just for Christmas Eve. I don't want you humbugging all over the house and scaring away Santa."

The bottle she was bringing to her mouth paused and she glared at me. "Funny."

I grinned. "So, are you busy? Want to come with?"

"What I want, is to finish my paper and study for Friday's exam…and shower. Is it clean?"

"Yes."

"Thank you."

She breezed past me a moment later with a waft of vanilla in her wake. I had to admit, she really did smell nice for a cantankerous person.

℃

Despite my efforts to bring Olivia with me, she refused and said she had plans. I was dubious. Traveling home a couple of days before Christmas, I called the apartment phone soon after I arrived.

"Hello, Olivia Boyd speaking, how may I help you?"

Ugh. Her phone manner was horribly polite. "Hi."

"Darcy?" she asked after a pause.

"Yep."

"Did you forget something?"

"No. Accidental dial I'm afraid. Sorry to bother you."

"It's fine. Goodbye."

"Wait."

"What?"

"You haven't left yet? I thought you were heading to the Bronx."

"I will be. Someone rang the apartment and held me up."

I scoffed and rolled my eyes. "Sorry," I said, not feeling that emotion in the slightest.

"Goodbye, Darcy."

The dial tone sounded in my ear. Suspicious, I considered ringing her back until my mother shouted out, "Taylor's here."

Smiling, I forgot the phone and ran outside to meet my friend. She enveloped me in a hug that lingered.

"You're home."

"I am."

She hesitated to pull away, and we were soon staring at one another with an uncomfortable charge between us.

"Umm...hi," I said, recalling the last conversation we had face to face.

"Hi."

"I've missed you."

"Me too."

She stepped back and looked over to the house. "Is Olivia here?"

I shook my head.

"Oh."

"Charli?"

"Went to Wisconsin to spend a couple of days with her brother's family."

"Oh." I had a full week at home, potentially time to spend one-on-one with Taylor. A luxury I hadn't had for months. A grin grew on my face and she mimicked it. "Slumber party?"

"I brought snacks."

We high-fived each other, and half an hour later, we were side-by-side in my bed watching the first in a long line of chick flick movies we planned to watch. Hands stuffed in a bowl of popcorn and candy, we munched away happily. It felt like old times.

"I missed this," I said around a mouthful of food.

"Me too, Charli hates these movies and never lets me eat in bed."

I choked on a piece of popcorn. *She slept with her?*

Taylor looked at me strangely then patted me on the back. "You okay?"

"Yeah." I coughed a little more. "I'm fine." Taking a long drink of soda, I settled back into my pillow and said nonchalantly. "So, you've slept together?"

"Umm…yeah."

"Oh."

"What? You think it's too soon?"

Absolutely! She had been an *out* bisexual for a microsecond and already had more action with a woman than I have in my ten years of lesbianism. "She's your girlfriend," I said, shrugging and trying not to sound spiteful. "I guess it was going to happen eventually."

"It did. Just after Thanksgiving, actually."

"Oh?"

"This is weird, isn't it?" Taylor asked as an awkward silence filled by Rachel McAdams fawning over some boy echoed into the room from the TV.

I took a deep breath. "Sort of."

Taylor turned to look at me, crossing her legs and looking serious. "I don't want to be weird around you. How do we get past this?"

I shrugged and mirrored her position. On the twin mattress, we were both precariously balanced on the edge.

She reached out and took my hand. "I'm sorry about the way I acted last time. Olivia was a bit left field." At my frown, she expanded on her words. "You coming home with a girlfriend was a shock."

I nibbled at my lip.

"It makes sense now."

"What does?" I frowned wondering how *any* of this made sense. I was sitting in my bed with the girl I had wanted for ten years, but couldn't stop feeling like I was cheating on Olivia. Figure that one out.

"You've never told me anything about anyone you had a crush on."

"That's because I only ever liked…" *Here we go.* "You. You and Olivia."

Taylor's eyes widened and she gaped a little. "But what about all that stuff we used to say about Jack and that dreamy exchange student, Antonio? Why did you say those things if you didn't mean them?"

I sighed. "I said those things to fit in, I guess. If you haven't noticed, the kids at school weren't all that tolerant. Look how they used to treat Marcus. He was a straight kid that loved to wear pink, but your boyfriend Jack and the rest were horrid to him."

"I haven't had any issues since dating Charli."

I nodded and looked at my lap.

"You know," Taylor said. "Since I *came out*, everyone has been asking if I used to date you."

I shook my head at the notion.

"Jack thinks it's awesome and said if we were ever up for a threesome…"

I grimaced. "Gross."

"I know, right?"

Nodding, I sighed. "So…you're bisexual now?"

Taylor shrugged. "I suppose."

"How did that happen?"

"Charli just…I don't know. She *did* something to me. She's beautiful. Sexy. Confident. She stated in her interview that she was gay and asked if that would be an issue. Since then…" Taylor shrugged. "I got curious."

I knitted my eyebrows together. "This is an experiment?"

Taylor huffed out a breath. "At the beginning…yeah. I guess. Now, though." She shrugged a shoulder. "Being with a woman is so different. They're softer, more tender, and well, you know, they know how to touch me. Guys are all fumbling and hopeless. At least, the guys at college were. And Jack." Taylor chuckled a little. "He had no idea what he was doing."

"But Charli does?"

Taylor nodded and studied my flat expression. "God, I'm sorry. This is weird, isn't it?"

"No," I said quickly. "I'm just trying to figure out how you went from raging heterosexuality to lesbian sex."

"I wasn't a raging hetero?"

That made me laugh. Taylor had a diary filled with her conquests. At last count, it was eight. I guess Charli made it nine. "What's it like?"

"What?"

I cleared my throat and fidgeted a little. "Sex."

Taylor cocked her head at me. "You've never had sex? Still?"

I shook my head.

"But Olivia…?"

"We, ah…we're still, umm…taking it slow?"

"But you've kissed her."

I nodded. How could I forget? She was an incredible kisser. "Yeah."

"But nothing else?"

I shook my head.

"Do you want to?"

I bit my lip as I thought about Olivia and I naked together. My body suddenly felt hot. "We'd probably argue the whole time," I said in response. Something that probably wouldn't be far from the truth. "She's irritating nearly a hundred percent of the time. She probably makes love like she lives life. Strict, controlled and *damn it, Darcy, I must orgasm now! What's taking you so long?*"

Taylor tipped her head back and laughed. I joined in as the whole idea of that situation amused me.

"Why are you with her?" Taylor asked when she calmed herself.

The smile fell from my face. *This is where you insert the truth, Darcy.* "I don't know. I just am."

"You're nuts. I'd suggest finding yourself someone better, but the way you two were at Thanksgiving…" Taylor blew out a breath and shook her head. "It was kinda something. It…"

"It?"

She shifted a little. "It made me kinda jealous."

"I noticed."

Taylor averted her eyes and blushed. She huffed out some air and looked at my Melissa Etheridge shrine on my dressing table. "I wonder what would have happened between us if you'd said something earlier."

"About Olivia?"

"No." Taylor shook her head. "About the lesbian thing. You had a crush on me. We could've…" She shrugged a shoulder.

A crush? The understatement of the century. I blushed and nodded. "I did." Past tense. I frowned a little. She leaned in and kiss my cheek, her mouth staying inches from my skin when she pulled back.

"I wish you'd told me this years ago. I can't help but want to know what it's like to kiss you."

I licked my lips and nodded again. "Yeah," I said with a choke. I *had* thought of it years ago. I would have given anything to show Taylor how much I loved her.

"I would have been safe experimenting with you."

I pulled away from her. "What?"

"What?" she said, confused at the way I raised my voice.

"I'm a safe option to *experiment* with?"

Her forehead scrunched. "Of course you would be. You're my best friend. We'd keep each other's secrets."

My chest tightened.

"And…you know, I'd know whether what I had with Charli was real or a phase."

I blinked incredulously at her. Who was this woman that was talking as if my feelings in this situation were perfectly adequate for a trial run? Taylor must have finally understood my expression because she gasped loudly.

"No! God, no. Sweetie, I wasn't belittling you. I mean, you're with Olivia. I meant I wished we had kissed back when there were no complications. No girlfriends to think about. I wasn't trying to suggest *you'd* be a phase." She looked imploringly at me as I swallowed. "Darce, please. I'm sorry. I didn't mean that like it sounded. I love you, sweetie. I'm just not *in* love with you. Not like I am with—" Taylor gasped.

"You love Charli," I said, stating the plain fact.

"Yeah, I think I do." Taylor sounded bewildered. "Oh my God."

And with those little words, what was left of my romantic feelings for Taylor ended like a test missile. Blowing up nothing but a pile of dirt leaving a big scar in the ground, only in this case, it was my heart.

∞

I rang Olivia's cell the next morning when Taylor went home to change. We had spent the night watching movies and eventually fell asleep side by side. Or, at least, *she* slept. I spent the night being creepy and watching her trying to figure out where my heart sat now. Limbo was my best guess.

I could see the faint scar on her eyebrow from when we both fell down a thinly covered snow slope. I longed to trace it with my finger, but I didn't want to wake her. The scar reminded me of all the good times we had shared together. We had been through everything. Family grief as our grandparents, or beloved pets passed. And about that one summer we feuded, resulting in the worse two days of my life. We had promised never to let our dissimilar tastes in music come between us again, despite the fact that New Kids on the Block broke up and my preferred band, U2, still existed.

"Hello?" Olivia answered, sounding like she was in the bottom of a tin can.

"Hi there."

"Oh, it's you."

76

I smiled. "Yep. How are you?"

"As well as could be expected when being interrupted at the laundromat."

Ah, that explained the tinny sounds. *Wait, why was she doing washing?* "Aren't you away with…whoever you're supposed to be visiting?" I made a note to ask who the heck she was going to see one day.

"Postponed until tomorrow."

"Why?"

"Weather." I heard a door close, presumably a dryer door, and she said, "Was there a purpose to this phone call, or did you just want to interrogate me?"

"Taylor slept over last night. She told me she loved Charli."

I could practically hear Olivia roll her eyes. "What has that got to do with me?"

"It's over."

"What is?"

"Everything."

Olivia sighed heavily. "Darcy, you're making no sense."

"Taylor and me, we're over."

"It's *Taylor and I*, and what do you mean you're over? Aren't you best friends anymore?"

"Yes."

Olivia groaned. "Then *what* is over?"

"She's not in love with me. *That's* what's over. My dreams and hopes have been shot down. I've nothing left and no one to love." I was smirking at the end of my rant.

"God. So dramatic."

I sighed and said, "Love is hard."

"Tell me about it."

"How does love work? How do you make someone fall in love with you?"

"I think the point is that you don't make anyone do anything. If it happens, it happens. Even when you wished it wouldn't."

I nodded my head. "Like me falling for Taylor you mean?"

"No, but that's a good example."

That was a curious answer. "Have you fallen for someone that didn't love you back?"

After a long pause, Olivia said, "I wasn't implying I had experience with the matter."

Lie. I grinned. "Who did you fall for?"

Olivia huffed at me. "I really haven't got time for gossip. Unless you've got important news, then I suggest you go play with your friend."

"I wish," I said with a chuckle and had the dial tone ringing in my ear a moment later. Olivia hung up on me. *Rude.*

∞

I saw as much of Taylor as I could over the holidays, and it felt like high school and university all over again. We walked through the snow, went skiing at the lodge and sat by the fire talking the day away. It felt like old times.

Right up to Christmas Day.

Charli came back.

She arrived on Taylor's arm, along with Taylor's parents, who came around and joined us for Christmas dinner just like they do every year. Taylor's house was smaller than ours, so with Mom and Dad's renovated dining room, we became the official Thanksgiving and Christmas venue decades ago. Mr. and Mrs. Robbins, Ed and Catrina, questioned Olivia's whereabouts.

"She couldn't make it," I told them, noticing Charli's smug face at hearing that news. She may be physically attractive, but she was a little too competitive and conceited for my liking. I was thrilled when she left after dinner citing an early morning at work. I was fed up with her kissing Taylor's neck at every opportunity. I wasn't jealous of it, but it was a little overdone. Taylor didn't look all that comfortable about it either. I mumbled 'Get a room' at them one time. Charli had winked and Taylor looked embarrassed. Charli didn't leave soon enough, and the instant she did, I got my happy-go-lucky friend back.

Bellies full and the fire toasting up the house in the lounge, our respective parents settled in to watch a Bing Crosby movie while Taylor and I snacked on Christmas pies in the kitchen.

I tossed my fork I was demolishing pudding with in the sink. It was too cold to run at the moment, and I could feel my stomach bulging out over my pants. I poked at the flesh there. The damage wasn't too bad. Turning around and leaning against the counter, I found the bravery to say, "She's a bit…dominant, isn't she?"

Taylor licked her fingers and gave me a quizzical look. "Huh?"

"Charli."

Taylor thought about it for a moment then shrugged. "I guess. I haven't really noticed."

"How can you not? She's all over you."

"Careful, Darce. You're sounding jealous."

I shrugged this time. I couldn't tell if it was jealousy or protectiveness.

Taylor rounded the counter and walked up to me. "Are you in love with me?"

"Yeah, of course, I love you."

Taylor smiled and her blue eyes sparkled. "That's not what I asked."

I swallowed the lump of gravelly truth that wanted to reveal itself. "I'm not *in* love with you." *Not anymore.*

Taylor's eyes roamed my face for a visual clue that I was lying. Those eyes lingered on my lips for a while, and I couldn't help but lick them. I'm sure I still had a bit of pie there anyway.

"I have a present for you," she said, snatching my hand and pulling me forward.

I frowned. "Oh? But you got me that stethoscope keychain."

"I know. I have something else, too. Come upstairs with me?"

Nodding and wiping my mouth on a napkin, we trudged upstairs with an extra pound of pudding in our stomachs to make our legs work harder.

I smiled at her after she shut my bedroom door, assuming she was about to pull out a present. What she did instead was unexpected. Grabbing me by the face, Taylor pulled me in for a kiss. Shocked, I was motionless for a moment as her mouth moved over mine. Her lips nipped at me and her tongue insisted that it needed to gain entry into my mouth. Figuring I may as well go with it, I shut my eyes and parted my lips to find myself immediately assaulted by her tongue.

She tasted like strawberries.

She also moaned and took handfuls of my backside in her hands. That moan made me frown. It didn't sound right and no surge of lust followed it. While I was trying to decipher the difference between her moan and Olivia's, she pushed me against the door. That felt wrong too. In fact, the whole situation was awkward. "Wait," I said, pushing her off. "What are you doing?"

"Giving you what you want."

"Which is?"

"Me."

My chest burned, but not with desire as it should have been. It felt hollow and wrong. I felt like I was kissing my non-existent sister. What the hell had I been thinking? "No."

She frowned.

"I don't want you like this. Not anymore. Once, maybe, but now…" I shook my head. Now I felt like a low-life cheater.

"But I thought…?"

I shook my head and created space between us. "No, Taylor. I'm sorry, but this feels…wrong somehow."

"You want me to break up with Charli first?"

I shook my head. "I want you to be with the person you love, and I don't think that's me. I don't feel that way for you. I…" I scratched my head. "I did once, but…"

Taylor sighed and sat heavily on my bed. "God, I'm so stupid. This was my worst idea ever."

"It's not your best, no," I said, sitting next to her and patting her leg.

"I'm sorry, Darce," she said, covering my hand with her own. "I thought…God, I don't know what I thought. Can you forgive me?"

"Always." I leaned over and kissed her on the cheek. "First and foremost, you're my best friend, and I never want to lose that."

"Will you tell Olivia?"

I nodded and she gasped.

"Seriously?"

I took in a deep breath and let it out with a rush. "There's something I need to tell you." And like all bad ideas, I confessed the truth about my fraudulent relationship with Olivia.

"You *used* me!" Taylor yelled five minutes later. "Worst still, you used her! Jesus, Darcy, what the hell is wrong with you?"

I had my head buried in my hands before she started yelling. "I just wanted to know if you were interested in me."

"By coming out and pretending to have a girlfriend?" Taylor bared her teeth. "That's a freaking despicable way to find out. Ever thought of asking like a normal person?"

I stood and uncovered my face. "A million times, but I didn't, because losing you would have been worse than hearing you didn't feel the same way."

Taylor stepped up to me and practically growled, "I would *never* walk away from our friendship, and you should have known that." She began to pace around the room. I swear she was snorting smoke out of her nose. "Thanksgiving was one big set up, wasn't it? Were you satisfied to find out I got jealous? Shit, Darcy, you made me look like a fool. I just about threw myself at you a second ago."

"I know, and I'm sorry. I just…" I withheld excuses. "I'm sorry."

"And Olivia...just how the hell did you get the weirdo to go along with this ridiculous plan."

"First, stop calling her names, secondly..." I cleared my throat. "I promised to clean the bathroom and cook for the rest of the year. Oh, and do laundry."

Taylor raised an eyebrow at me. A very unimpressed one. "You're kidding me? She came up here to meet your parents, your *love* interest, and even *kissed* you, just so you'd cook and clean?"

When put like that it did sound like a whole lot of sacrifice for very little reward. "Yes?"

Taylor narrowed shrewd-looking eyes. "She likes you, doesn't she?"

"Likes me?" I burst out laughing. "Oh, yeah, I'm her favorite person *ever*. She just loves me." I kept chuckling, but at Taylor's continued silence, I stopped. "No, Tay. She doesn't like me."

Taylor cocked her head and smirked. She wouldn't explain that look, and left, making me promise to never do anything as low again, and demanded I apologize to Olivia.

∞

I went to bed that night feeling like a monster. I had become the Scrooge of relationships. Taylor was right. I used her, I used Olivia, and I even used Charli, just to find out if I could make Taylor jealous. The answer was yes, but I got no satisfaction from it. I got nothing but a bucket load of guilt that didn't mix well with the amount of Christmas pie I ate.

Rubbing at my churning stomach, and unable to sleep, I reached my hand out into the cold air and snatched my phone from the side table.

"Darcy?" Olivia said, answering.

"Hi."

"Why are you calling?"

"Accidental dial."

Silence.

Chuckling, I said, "I called to say Merry Christmas. Did you have a good day?"

Her answer hesitated. "It was like any other Christmas, I suppose."

Having no idea what that meant, I asked, "So what did you do today? Was Santa kind to you?"

"I visited some people and ate roast chicken, and I don't believe in Santa."

"Wow...thrilling," I said, rolling my eyes.

"How are your parents?"

"They're good. They asked where you were. So did Taylor and Charli." Olivia didn't respond. "She kissed me."

"What? Who did?"

"Taylor kissed me. Sort of."

"Oh." She paused. "Congratulations are in order, I suppose."

"Mmm. I guess."

"Was that not what you wanted?"

"Yeah, but it wasn't a happy ending."

"She's a bad kisser?"

"Uh..." I couldn't help but compare Olivia's kiss to Taylor's one from the moment it happened. There was a clear victor if I had to be the judge of the best female kisser of the year. It broke my heart to know that it wasn't my best friend that would emerge the victor. "She tried to seduce me."

Silence. Then, "You are aware she has a girlfriend?"

"Very."

"So did you let her?"

"Seduce me? No." I took a deep breath and sighed. "She's in love with Charli."

"So what is she doing trying to get into your pants?"

"She...uh...was trying to give herself to me as a present."

"Excuse me?"

"Umm..."

Olivia scoffed. "Why you have a crush on a clearly emotionally-challenged woman is completely lost on me."

I sighed. It seems crushing on unavailable women was my thing. *First Taylor, then Olivia*, I thought. I gasped and shook my head. *No. Not possible.* Swallowing my wayward thoughts, I changed tack. "She asked if we'd slept together."

"As if that's any of her business."

I smirked. That was an odd response. "I told her no."

Olivia scoffed.

"What?"

"I'm surprised you didn't say we did it three times a day. Apparently you have no problems sullying your morals, but when it comes to your virtue, you're sickeningly pure."

"My morals aren't sullied, thank you very much."

"Faking that you have a girlfriend to make your best friend, who also has a girlfriend, jealous. No, that sounds perfectly reasonable."

I scowled into the phone. "Okay, so they're a little...dented."

"Train wreck, more like."

"Fine. Whatever. None of it matters anymore anyway. She knows the truth."

"That you're a coward hiding behind a lie?"

I took a deep breath. "Yes. I told her that I used you to make her jealous."

Olivia was quiet for a moment. "Oh?" Olivia cleared her throat quietly. "Good. I hope you made it clear you blackmailed me into it. I'm not having my reputation tarnished because of your pathetic plan."

I sighed. "Yes, she's aware it was my stupid plan. She's already lectured me and demanded I apologize to you."

"Well, don't let me stop you."

I pinched the bridge of my nose. I felt a headache coming on. "I'd prefer to do it in person. I'll see you in a couple of days."

"Can't wait," she purred sarcastically.

"Night, honey-bun," I said, poking the wounded bear.

I could practically hear her grimace and then she hung up on me.

Chuckling, I tucked my phone under my pillow and drifted off to sleep.

Chapter Seven

In my bag was the most precious possession I owned, and now, it was about to be the only peace offering I thought would be good enough. Returning to Boston on New Year's Eve, I arrived back at the apartment just before the sun set.

"Honey, I'm home," I called out as I bustled my way into the flat.

"Oh, hurray," came the flat response from somewhere in the apartment.

I frowned and looked around for my sullen roommate. "Olivia?"

"Yes?"

Yelping, I clutched at my chest in fright, Olivia having popped up from behind the kitchen counter. "God, I hope you remember CPR, you nearly gave me a heart attack."

"I'm surprised you haven't already suffered one from all the rubbish you ingest."

"I don't eat junk food *all* the time."

She gave me a dubious glare.

Letting my head fall forward as I grunted in frustration, I gave myself a big cheery *welcome home* in my head and trudged to my bedroom. The old leather case I retrieved from my bag could wait until Olivia wasn't being…well…*Olivia*. Peace offerings required a certain mood, and like hell I was going to hand her something precious while she was being a facetious bovine.

හ

"Are you doing anything special tonight?" I asked Olivia when she finished her evening meal of ravioli. I munched on my takeaway Thai curry waiting for her to answer.

"It's just another night."

"It's New Year's Eve." I picked up my beer and toasted her before washing down a mouthful of food. "Want some beer?" I asked for the second time.

"I still don't drink."

"So you said, but it's New Year's Eve." She glared at me. I gave up. "So…" I started after we had cleaned up after finishing our respective dinners. "What do you usually do on New Year? Do you stay up? Watch the fireworks on TV? Go to bed early?"

"I read."

Of course she did. "Oh? What do you read? Anatomy textbooks?" I asked, trying to sound interested as I shot the TV with the remote. It came to life and I quickly muted it.

"A book," she said as she entered the bathroom.

I looked over at her and put down the instructions for my new wireless headphones my parents got me for Christmas. "A book?"

"Yes."

"Called…?"

She didn't answer as the sound of her brushing her teeth came from the bathroom. After rinsing and turning off the tap, she said as she emerged, "None of your business."

I rolled my eyes. "Sounds like a thrilling read."

"It is. Good night."

"Night. Happy New Year."

She gave me a weary look and closed her bedroom door. I sneered at the wooden barrier for a moment. *Why did I have to say sorry to her again?*

My movie finished just shy of midnight. It was a motivational rom-com about second chances and friendship and family and all the mushy stuff that warmed the cockles of the heart. Packing away the headphones and flicking over to the live feed from New York, I grabbed another beer and noticed Olivia still had the light on in her room.

Biting my lip, I decided it was time.

Putting down my bottle, I retrieved the leather bag from my room and knocked softly on her door. I had no intentions of making a loud banging noise in case she was asleep, lights and all.

"Yes?" her muted voice called out.

I cracked open the door and poked my head around. "Hi. Can I come in for a moment?"

She sighed. "If you must." She put her book down after checking the page number and I glanced at the title.

"Harry Potter? Seriously?" The look on her face told me to shut the hell up or I'll be sorry. "Anyway," I said quickly. "Umm...here." I handed her the bag. "I want to thank you for pretending to be my girlfriend. That, and I wanted to give you something for Christmas. You know...because it's the season to give and all that." I tapped on the case. "I thought of you when I saw this." And I had. Rummaging through my closet for my snow shoes, I had found the worn case and thought of how much Olivia would appreciate the contents. If anyone was geeky enough to cherish this, it was her. "Anyway. It's yours. Merry Christmas and thank you and sorry."

She looked at the bag warily. "It's a doctor's bag," she said, stating the obvious.

"Yes. From the eighteen hundreds. Open it."

She did...carefully. Inside were restored instruments of a nineteenth-century surgeon. It had been my pride and joy for nearly two decades. After saving Taylor's life when she was a child, the doctor gave it to me as a reward, complimenting me on my cool head and encouraging me to consider medicine in my future. Since then, the bag had been my talisman to achieve that goal.

Olivia's hand had covered her mouth when she saw what was inside. "It's beautiful."

"I know," I said, tracing my finger over one of the old ivory-handled scalpels.

"I can't. It's too much."

I shook my head and stilled the hands she was using to push the bag back at me. "No, it's just enough. You helped shield my fears from my friend while giving me the courage to try and express my feelings for her. You didn't have to come to Minnesota, but you did, and for that, I'm grateful."

"You told her how you felt?"

I lowered my gaze. "Yeah. It was about then that she admitted she was in love with Charli, and I realized I didn't feel the same about her anymore."

"So why did she try to seduce you?"

I laughed wryly through my nose. "Who knows. I didn't get around to asking because she was too busy tearing me a new one."

Olivia shook her head and looked once again at the surgery kit. "I can't accept this."

"Yes, you can."

She shook her head even more adamantly. "No. You can barely afford food, I won't let you give me a gift that's clearly worth—"

"I didn't buy it for you. I've had that kit for nearly twenty years."

"You've had this since you were a child?"

I nodded. "Yes. And now I'm giving it to you. No returns."

Olivia bit her lip and looked at the bag longingly. "It is beautiful."

I smiled. "Yes." The sound of soft cheers from the TV reached us, and the soft pop of fireworks from outside permeated the walls. "Happy New Year."

Olivia smiled at me. Not one of those carnivorous ones to placate me, but a genuine smile complete with shining eyes. It was beautiful. I was definitely a little bit in lust with her. Just my luck. "Happy New Year," she said in return, her eyes lingering on mine.

I leaned in and heard her breath hitch. "What are you doing?" she asked as I paused a few inches from her mouth.

"Kissing you?"

"Why?"

"Because it's New Year. It's tradition."

She put her hands on my chest and shoved. "I don't think so." And just like that, the mood popped.

Raking my hand through my hair and realizing my pulled back style was an abysmal mess from laying on the couch, I stood and huffed. "Fine. Good night."

She was staring at me as I looked back when I closed the door, a thoughtful expression on her face. Tired and unwilling to try and decipher it, I took myself to bed.

℘

We had five days left of the Christmas break, and then it was back to the medical grindstone. Quickly, I was knee-deep in policy, epidemiology and back to doing patient-doctor rounds. Before Christmas, I did my rounds with three other potential doctors. One girl, Susan Childs, had a tendency to throw up whenever a patient did, and she often squealed when handling organs during our anatomy classes. I wasn't surprised to find that Susan hadn't come back to Harvard Medical School. What did surprise me was the loss of eight other students for reasons we speculated on over lunch. Financial difficulties and a change of heart were the front-runners. In one case, there was a rumor a student won the lotto and retired overseas at the tender age of twenty-six. I was smiling about that when our new patient-doctor groups were allocated thanks to the drop in numbers.

I was still in a group with Olivia. *Great.* Miss Pedantic herself. After previously spending time watching how the patient inquiries were done, and being allowed to ask simple questions, this time, we were upgrading to doctor interrogation level.

Knowing there was nothing I could do about watching Olivia boss her way through her patient inquiries, I stood back and prepared to grimace when Dr. Fredricks asked her to talk to the first patient on our rounds.

She was a little old lady with cute curly hair. Poor innocent victim number one.

"Good morning," Olivia said to her. "How are you today Mrs. Lindsay?"

"My stomach hurts like a bitch, my head is pounding and I have cramp in my ass. How do you think I am?" Mrs. Lindsay said with a scowl. Feisty woman.

I looked around to the rest of my training group. Henriquez Paolo, a man with a Spanish accent, snickered into his doctor's coat. The other woman, new to our group and rather attractive, looked at me and winked. I flushed but managed a smile back at her before watching the drama unfold at the bedside.

"Have you had pains like this before?" Olivia asked.

"Yes, every time I eat that idiotic man's fish stew." She pointed to a man trying to blend into the cubicle curtains. "That ain't nothing but poison, you silly old coot. Mamma's secret recipe, you say. What'd she use it for? To top off your old man?"

The man poked his tongue out at his wife. Useful.

Olivia looked at her chart. "You've been suffering from diarrhea and vomiting since last night?"

"Yes. Thanks to his efforts to kill me."

Olivia ignored the bitter woman's accusations. "I suspect, Mrs. Lindsay, that you have an intolerance to something in the dish. You're severely dehydrated, so I suggest we put you on fluids, give you something for the nausea and something to relax the muscles in your rectum."

"My what?"

Olivia leaned forward and said, "Your ass, Mrs. Lindsay."

"Oh. Well, why didn't you just say that? All that fancy doctor talk is just showing off. I ain't dumb, lady!"

Olivia smiled at the undeserving woman. A smile that had me copying her. It wasn't one of those sneers often directed at me, but something warm and caring. I didn't think she had it in her. "We'll have you fighting fit in no time, however, I suggest you avoid the fish stew in future. I also highly recommend you study the ingredients in it and pinpoint which one you react to just in case you get more than a case of food poisoning next time."

We left Mr. and Mrs. Lindsay to the argument that ensued after those suggestions and continued our rounds. Each time we did patient-doctor inquiries after that, Olivia proved to me each and every time that she was going to be a remarkable doctor. She was by far the winner of the bedside manner competition. The fact that she correctly diagnosed everyone had her ranked at the top of the class. She was a show off with a multiple personality disorder.

∞

The new girl in our rotation group was Kara Adelman and she had a winking fetish. At least, that's what I figured because she winked at me quite often over the next few weeks. Her hair was flame-red and clearly out of a bottle, and her eyes mismatched it by being dark brown. Her skin was pale and freckly, but by no means unattractive. Especially with those short skirts she wore in direct opposition to the frigid weather. Her legs were marvelous and she had noticed me look at them more than once. *Mortifying.*

In anatomy lab, she was in the group at the gurney beside the group Olivia and I were in, and often I'd look up to see her watching me. I couldn't decide whether it was creepy or flattering.

"Will you pay attention?" Olivia had hissed at me once, moving into my sight line and making me realize I'd been staring at Kara for longer than socially acceptable. Olivia's annoyance of me paying Kara attention had been escalating for weeks, and she'd been intercepting a lot of our silent exchanges. Taylor was right, she was controlling. My eyes took a familiar road over her body when she went back to studying Dolores' heart. Olivia had worn a very low-cut top today, and in retrospect, they had been getting lower by the day. I looked up just in time to catch Olivia giving me the evil eye. I'm sure she's going to smother me in my sleep eventually. In fact, I was positive she would when, once again, I had landed firmly on her bad side. "What?" I had snapped back at her once in a whisper on our patient rounds. Olivia was giving me the displeased look because, once again, I was caught looking at Kara's legs...by both women. "I'm being friendly."

Olivia had pulled me up as Kara, Susan, Henriquez and Dr. Fredricks moved onto the next patient. "You're being a distinct perv."

I burst out laughing and quickly reigned the noise in as a nurse walked past glaring at me. "I am *not* a hussy," I whispered back.

"Are you really that deprived of intimacy, that you're now throwing yourself at anyone that looks interested?"

"Excuse me, I am doing no such thing."

"Then give the fuck-me eyes a rest. No one needs to be witness to your descent into appalling desperation, and I'm tired of protecting you."

Olivia stormed off leaving me utterly shocked that she even knew how to swear.

Shocked that I was, it took me a good five minutes to say, "Wait, protecting me from what?" I looked around at the empty corridor for answers. The unused gurney and IV stand offered no clues.

∽

"Hi," Kara said one gray afternoon in early February as she climbed the low stone wall marking the quadrangle grass.

"Ah...hi?" I said, my sandwich halfway to my mouth.

"May I sit with you?" Kara asked me as she parked herself on the grass in the quadrangle where I usually ate my lunch.

"Sure."

"Kara," she said, holding out her hand.

Mine were sticky from the peanut butter and jelly oozing from my sandwich, so I grimaced apologetically and said, "I know. We do inquiries together, and basically every single first-year course."

She smiled. Perfect white teeth all beautifully lined up. It was a stunning smile. "And you're Darcy Wright."

"I am." I grinned.

"It feels silly that we waited seven months to introduce ourselves properly," Kara said. She was right. A lot of the other med students met up socially and studied in groups together. I had Olivia to study with, and really, that's all any prospective doctor needed. Socially, I couldn't afford to do much, so I scrimped and saved my dry cleaning coins for cheap beer that Olivia scowled at when I drank it. "Hello?" Kara said, her hand was waving in front of my face.

"Hi. Sorry, I zoned out. You're right, it's strange we haven't really *met* before. I mean, you're in our rotation group now, so really, we should have said hi before now…right?"

She smiled at my rambling.

"Well, now we have, and I must say, it's an absolute pleasure." She smiled and touched my forearm, an action that set alarms off in my head.

Oh, hell, was that a come on, or just a friendly gesture? Not having any clue what to do, I stuffed my sandwich in my mouth and nodded my head.

"So, where are you from Dr. Wright?" Kara asked with a crooked smile.

"Minnesota."

"Do you have anyone waiting at home for you?"

I frowned. "Uh…my parents?"

Kara giggled. A full-on genuine high-pitched giggle. It made me fidget. "No, I meant a *significant* other."

"Oh…" I thought of Taylor by pure reflex. That ship had long sailed. I sighed and looked away. I spotted Olivia scowling at me from the benches near the building. *Ugh, now what had I done?* I chomped down hard on my sandwich and glared back at her. Around a mouthful of food, I mumbled, "No, there's no significant other."

Kara soaked that information up and her eyes scanned the quadrangle to follow my gaze. She frowned and cocked her head at something. "What about her?" Kara asked when she noticed I had spotted Olivia.

My sandwich got stuck in my throat "*Olivia?*" I managed to choke out when I cleared my airway.

"Yeah, you two seem to have a…thing."

"A thing?" I shook my head vigorously. "No. No *thing*. I mean, we kissed that one time, but no, nothing else." *Christ, why did I say that?*

"You *kissed* her?"

"Well, technically, she kissed me."

Kara stared at me for a moment. "Let me get this straight…sort of. You're a lesbian?"

"I…what?" *Oh my, God, I'd totally outed myself to a stranger.* Fearful of her response I tried smiling. I could see from her reaction it didn't look convincing.

"Forgive me for being forward, but I find that I don't really have time to waste chasing the wrong skirt, if you know what I mean? With the amount of time we need to study, I need to know straight up if I'm even in with a shot." She gave Olivia a side-long glance.

I had no idea what she meant and nor could I formulate a response.

Kara waited for my reaction for a short time before blushing…a lot. "I got it all wrong didn't I?"

"Wrong?"

"Well, I've been watching you this past few weeks, not in a creepy way I might add, but you just seem…I've seen the way you look at women."

I blinked. "How do I look at women?"

"You look at them with more interest than is usual for a straight girl."

"I do?"

Kara nodded. "Her especially," she said, looking back over at Olivia.

I would have laughed if I wasn't so shocked. *Since when do I look at Olivia?* It was Kara I was getting into trouble for looking at. "Olivia? That woman drives me insane. She's my roommate."

"You *live* with her?"

I nodded. "She's neurotic. She's a great teacher, though."

"Teacher?"

"She's teaching me how to cook."

"Oh." Kara didn't seem to know what to do with that information. She started packing up her lunch and stood. "I'm sorry for coming on so strong. I don't usually get so muddled."

"Wait." I rushed to my feet. "Yes."

"Yes, what?"

"I'm gay. Have been since forever."

Kara smiled. It looked like a victorious grin. "May I sit with you in the next class?"

"Absolutely." A smile stayed with me most of the way to class. I had a feeling I'd just successfully flirted with, and potentially picked up, my first woman. Noticing Olivia's scowl as Kara sat beside me wiped the grin right off my face. *Oh, hell.*

Chapter Eight

"I see you made a friend," Olivia said later that week as she guided me through the technique to make pizza dough. She had decided she was fed up with me ordering the junk food and decided it was high time I learned how to make it myself.

"Who? Kara?" I said, washing flour from my hands.

"She's been your shadow since Monday."

"She's just being friendly," I said, rolling out the dough as I was instructed. "She asked if she can study with me."

"I bet she did," Olivia muttered under her breath. "Stop!" she said to me next. "You're massacring the dough. Get it back into a ball and try again...gently this time."

I did as I was told. This time I successfully rolled out a perfect pizza base. Sort of. It was a little elliptical, but I figured it would still taste like pizza in the end. Next we tipped on the tomato sauce Olivia had made me make from scratch. It was yummy.

"Okay, now assemble the toppings, sprinkle with cheese, and put it in the oven."

Following the instructions, I stood back proudly and watched my pizza bake. "How long does it cook for?"

"Twelve to fifteen minutes. Depends on the oven. So, what did you say?"

"Huh?"

"To Kara about studying together?"

"Oh...I said maybe we could catch up at the library sometimes. I didn't think you'd want her here, and to be honest, I prefer to study with you anyway."

Olivia looked at me for an extended moment. "Okay then," she said with a short nod. "Don't forget to keep an eye on your pizza as you clean up." She promptly left the kitchen and shut herself in her room. I rolled my eyes at her. *So weird.*

☙

"This is lovely," Kara said a few days later as we soaked in the spring sun. The grass had dried out, and while it was brown and crispy, it was still suitable to lounge about on. We'd just finished our morning lecture on the respiratory system. She had sat beside me since the day she introduced herself. It was nice not to sit by myself. Kara had a tendency to whisper a lot, but I figured the company made up for the distraction from the lecturer.

"Yeah," I said, opening my water bottle. It wouldn't come off. Groaning with effort, I was forced to concede defeat. Dehydration was in my future.

"Here," Kara said with a chuckle as she watched my efforts. She twisted the top off with ease.

"I loosened it," I said as she handed it back.

"No, I work out." She took my hand and put it on her arm as she flexed it. "See?"

"Uh…" I nodded.

She smiled that perfect smile again and pulled my hand from her arm.

Over the course of the past week or so, I found out that Kara was Texan and from a wealthy ranching family. She had a brother at Yale doing law, and another in the fourth year at John Hopkins Medical School. She was a very smart and very good looking woman. She had also told me she was a lesbian halfway through a lecture on medical policy. I had choked on my gum, which started me coughing and earned me whispered 'shut it' from Olivia, who sat behind me. I looked over my shoulder and glared at her. Since Kara had begun sitting beside me, I had noticed Olivia's seat placement had crept closer to mine. She informed me when I confronted her about it that the acoustics behind my regular seat were optimum for hearing the professor…when Kara wasn't constantly whispering to me, that is.

"So, Darcy, I've established you're single, you're planning to get your General Practitioners license, you've never had a relationship, and that you throw all your love at a car stored in your dad's shed."

"Uh…yeah?" Kara was an expert question-asker and sometimes, I almost felt like I was being interrogated. Her pretty smile and twinkling dark eyes made up for it, though. Kara was tall, slim, and probably looked terrific without her clothes on. I blushed as that thought crossed my mind, hoping like crazy she couldn't mind read.

Kara reached over and interlaced our fingers. I gulped.

"A few of us are meeting at the bar tonight. Will you come with me?"

"I…" I faltered. I had a shift at Sunny's and wasn't being paid until next Thursday. The life on a student wage was a frugal one.

Kara cocked an eyebrow.

I didn't want to tell the rich woman that I was working for minimum wage cleaning dubious stains off clothes. "I can't really afford to this week. Can we rain check it?"

Kara smiled and shook her head as my pathetic financial situation was revealed. "Oh, sweetie, you don't have to pay for anything. It's on me." Kara lifted my hand and kissed the knuckles. Wow…that was rather sexy.

"Am I interrupting something?" Olivia said as she appeared out of nowhere.

I yanked my hand out of Kara's softer one. "It wasn't me!" I said and shut my eyes to groan. Why did I say that?

Olivia cocked her head at me then smirked. "Is that your go-to guilty response?"

I scowled and rubbed at the ache forming in my stomach. I swear Olivia gave me stomach ulcers.

Kara was looking between the pair of us curiously. "Hi, I'm Kara," she said, holding her hand out to Olivia.

"I'm aware of that," Olivia said, ignoring the hand and nodding curtly instead. I rolled my eyes. "So, this is a cozy lunch," Olivia said. "Mind if I join you?" To my surprise, she sat down on the dried grass. *What happened to her adamant stance about how positively unrefined it was to sit on dirt?*

"Umm…" Kara said.

"Great." Olivia pulled out her rabbit food with feta cheese. "So…what are we talking about?"

"Drinks," I said.

"Oh? With whom?"

"Kara. She asked me to join her and some of the others at the bar tonight."

"Did she?" Olivia turned her shrewd gaze onto Kara. "Who else is going?"

"Ah…" Kara shrugged. "I won't know until we get there." Kara made a show of looking at her watch. "Damn. I wanted to run past the library before next session. I'd better hurry." She packed her things and stood. Looking at me, she touched my shoulder and said, "Please come tonight. My shout. I'll be there at nine."

Feeling I'd better do the polite thing when offered free drinks, I smiled and nodded. "Cool. See you later then." I'd also be done at work, too.

"What are you doing?" Olivia snapped when Kara was out of ear-shot.

"Nothing."

"You're holding hands and saying yes to a date. I'd say that's more than nothing."

"A date? That's not what this is."

"Oh, really? Christ, Darcy, how blind are you?"

"I'm not blind at all, thank you very much. I made a friend, deal with it."

"Kara has been flirting with you all year. I know you're inexperienced, but surely you can see that?"

I pouted and thought back to all the little touches Kara had given me. "So what?"

Olivia huffed. "You're clearly rebounding from your obsession with Taylor."

"I wasn't *obsessed* with Taylor."

Olivia scoffed. "You mentioned her every second of the day, and honestly, it's been a relief not to hear about it anymore."

"Yeah, well, I'm cutting my losses and moving on."

"Thank God. It's about time you did, but not with Kara."

I threw my hands up. "Why the hell not? She's apparently interested."

"And she'll be disinterested just as quickly. I asked around, Kara likes a challenge, but once she's had her fill, she moves on."

I scrunched my face up. "Don't be ridiculous."

"Don't be so naïve."

"And what the hell are you doing running about and investigating her? What sort of creeper move is that?"

Olivia rolled her shoulders and did her best to look impassive. "You're my roommate. I can't have people we hardly know stomping through the apartment. I pre-screened her for you."

"Pre-screened her? God, what does that even mean?" I shook my head and a thought popped into my head. "Wait. Did you screen me too?"

"Of course I did, though sometimes, I wonder if I should have asked for a psych evaluation first."

Making a frustrated grunting noise, I started shoving my belongings into my bag. "You're impossible, you know that?"

"Yes, I do, but I'm also stupid enough to try and protect you from the likes of Kara Adelman."

"I don't need protecting." I stood and rubbed at the cramp-like feeling in my gut.

"Yes, you do. I'm coming with you tonight. What's wrong with your stomach?"

"I don't need a chaperone." I tried to ignore the fact my voice was now whining like a child. "And *you* give me ulcers."

"Too bad. I'm coming anyway. I don't trust her. In fact, I don't trust you either. Consider me your wingman. Or woman."

"God. Whatever." I hoisted my bag onto my bag and skulked off.

"Stop eating so much grease."

"What?"

"Your stomach. Probably complaining about all the saturated fats you feed it."

I scowled. Olivia was exasperating.

ဆ

I arrived at the bar early, escaping my apartment before Olivia got out of the bathroom. I figured if I wasn't there when she came out, then she wouldn't come at all. I chuckled to myself at my brilliant plan, positive that Olivia really didn't care what I got up to, unless it was eating fried chicken on the couch. *That* she hated.

Victorious, I perched myself on a barstool and waited while subtly sniffing at my skin. I hadn't had a chance to shower myself, and something ripe and unsavory was all over a bag of clothes that I had to deal with earlier.

I should have showered.

"Can I get you something?" the bartender asked me.

"Thanks, I'll wait for my friend."

Then my *friend* walked through the door. *Wow.* Kara's hair was down and flowing in silky strands over her shoulders. She had tipped herself into a pair of skinny jeans and equally as skinny sequined top. I couldn't help but stare at the swell of her top, or the way her hips swayed. She was like a tempting piece of chocolate I wanted to unwrap and taste. Her movements were fluid, and I felt a nice rush of desire escalate through my skin. About to smile at her, I was distracted by the next person entering the bar.

Crap.

It was Olivia and I had no chance of preventing my jaw from dropping. I'd never seen her in anything but jeans and tops, and that one time with the towel, but this time, she was wearing a very short and very tight, little black dress. *Holy hell.* Kara's legs were something, but Olivia's were something else. Where Kara was temptation in tight pants, Olivia was just...*damn.* My mouth went dry when my eyes roamed over her body. I knew she was an attractive woman, I wasn't dead, but I didn't know she could look like *this.* She was everything anyone could ever want to feast on without the chocolate-induced cavities. I blushed a brilliant crimson when I wondered what she looked like under that tight piece of fabric.

Oh, hell in a handbasket. Stop undressing her. My eyes dropped down to her chest again. *And stop staring at her boobs!* Yet, try as I might, I couldn't take my eyes off her as she approached me with a smug grin on her face. *I'm in so much trouble.*

"Hi," she said breathlessly, taking me by surprise.

I vaguely noticed Kara's sour expression as I answered, "Uh..." *Smooth.*

Olivia leaned in and my breathing ceased entirely as she afforded me a view down her dress. Lace encased her breasts and it was taunting me with how I was allowed to look but not touch.   It was then that I recognized my rather large, unavoidable, and consuming crush I had on my roommate. *When the hell did that happen? Oh, crap. Oh, hell. Oh, my freaking God! This was such a bad idea.* "Huh?" I said, realizing that Olivia had asked me a question. I had to physically drag my eyes away from her cleavage.

Olivia just smiled at me and said, "About time."

The thing is, I don't think those words weren't referring to my inability to stop staring at her breasts. I'm positive they meant a whole lot more and I realized it had taken me far too long to catch up.

Everything made so much more sense now. The way I kept comparing Taylor to Olivia, and then Kara to Olivia. The way I did my best not to obsess on that kiss at Thanksgiving. The fact I rejected Taylor for her, and the way Olivia kept running interference on Kara's advances. Little things fell down on top of me like an avalanche of clues. Olivia always had something for me to eat after my late-night shifts at the dry cleaner. She did my laundry with hers, citing that it just made efficient sense, and even though that was supposed to be my job now, she said she didn't trust me and kept doing it anyway. Not once had she asked me for laundromat money. She even let me watch the Super Bowl with the sound on.

One doesn't do any of those things if you didn't care about someone, and considering Olivia's initial attitude toward me to the one she presented now, it was like knowing two separate people.

"Umm…what's going on here?" Kara said as Olivia's smile dropped away as though my silent response had deflated her confidence.

I looked at Kara briefly before looking back at Olivia, still bewildered by everything that had just rattled through my head. "I…umm…have to go." I hopped off my stool and ran for it, leaving Kara pouting and Olivia looking smug…again. I heard Olivia say 'I win' before I left the bar.

8ο

I shut myself in my room when I returned to the apartment. My stomach ache had increased exponentially on my walk home, which was a nice distraction from the confusion in my head. What was I thinking? Having a crush on Olivia was insane. Did she really like me back? Had I come to the right conclusion? Was that stunt with the black dress all about proving how naïve I was, or was it some sort of seduction attempt? I groaned at the idea of Olivia seducing me. I bet she would be amazing at it. Then my stomach cramped again and I groaned in pain. Thinking painkillers might help, I was about to search for some when I heard Olivia come back. Doubt reigned again. Convinced I'd misread the situation, and pretty certain Olivia tolerated my presence at best, I was unwilling to leave my sanctuary to face a gloating roommate. I was an easily infatuated, inexperienced fool. So instead, I curled up into a ball and grimaced as best I could.

It was after midnight when pain ripped through my side forcing me to cry out. I promised myself to never eat two-day-old Thai takeaway again as the pain refused to budge. I opened my eyes mid-grimace to find my vision blocked by a pair of legs encased in black tights. When had Olivia come into my room and where was that killer black dress? I trailed my eyes up to her crossed arms and frowning expression.

I whispered, "Hello."

"Hmm. Why are you making so much noise?"

"Wind."

Olivia's face scrunched up in distaste and she moved away. "Well then, could you keep the moaning to a minimum?"

I nodded.

She watched me for a moment longer through narrowed eyes as if assessing I was okay before moving off, leaving the door open.

I sighed in relief as the sounds of her typing on her laptop drifted in. That exchange was very normal for us, with no traces of awkward. Or gloating. *Victory.*

The pain refused to let go and gradually moved away from my stomach. A sudden lurch in my belly had me up-ending my reheated dinner all over the carpeted floor of my bedroom. As I coughed after emptying my stomach, I felt like a hot poker had just been stabbed into my side then jiggled around a bit. I cried out in a muffle while being sick. *Gross.*

Olivia was by my side in seconds with a damp towel to wipe my face. Guiding me away from the mess on the floor, she lay me back down on the bed. Pressing a hand to my head, she frowned.

"Where is the pain localized?" she asked, using the damp towel to wipe my brow.

"There," I said, clutching the area just beside my right hip.

"May I?" Olivia asked, tugging at the hem of my shirt.

I nodded and allowed her to move my hands out of the way while she lifted my sweater, shirt and t-shirt out of the way. I tried to remember if I had left my bra on. I hissed as her hands felt icy against my skin.

"Sorry," she said softly. She began to gently palpitate my stomach, moving slowly down towards my groin. I cried out when she released the pressure just above the right side of my pubic bone. She pulled my clothes back down and took hold of my hand. "Darcy, I'm going to call an ambulance, okay?"

I nodded, coming to the same diagnosis as Olivia. So much for bad Thai, my body was trying to kill me of its own accord.

Olivia didn't let go of my hand once she got off the phone, even when the paramedics arrived. Giving them a succinct account of my probable appendicitis, she rode in the ambulance with me to one of the hospitals affiliated with Harvard Medical School. There, a surgeon came to see me.

"Ah, Miss Wright and Miss Boyd," the man said to us. He was our teaching doctor from our Patient-Doctor course. "It's not often I get to operate on my own students," Dr. Fredricks said with a delighted chuckle. He sounded a little deranged. Looking at my chart, he declared, "Appendicitis."

I nodded as he confirmed the diagnosis for himself with a series of pokes and prods and a study of my ultrasound results.

"Acute appendicitis. Emergency surgery it is," he said proudly at the end. "Miss Boyd, perhaps you'd like to scrub in and assist?"

Olivia's jaw fell open. Curiously, she then turned to me. Why she didn't just scream out 'yes' is beyond me. "Would you mind?"

I shook my head. I just wanted the pain to end. I didn't care if Scooby-Do assisted Dr. Fredricks.

"Yes, sir, I'd be delighted to assist," she said.

"Very well, follow me. Miss Wright, we'll see you in OR momentarily."

I was wheeled into an operating room where I was surrounded by people in masks forced to listen to some classical noise being piped into the room.

"Hi," a masked person said before taking my hand. Olivia. I recognized the thin, slightly cool, but soft, fingers.

I gave her a weak smile. A clear mask was soon placed over my head, and the next thing I knew, I counted backward from ten and poof, I was waking up again.

"I called your parents."

I scrunched up my face and frowned. "Huh?"

Olivia's face came into view through the fuzzy veil of my eyes. I scrunched them tighter a few times to clear my vision. Olivia was smiling. "I called your parents and let them know you were okay."

"Thanks," I said, sort of. It came out sounding like Kermit with a sore throat.

"Here." Olivia put a sliver of ice in my mouth. "How do you feel?"

"Umm…good?"

Olivia smiled. It was nice to have her doctor-smile turned on me for once. It was really very lovely. Thoughts of her smiling like that in her black dress came to mind and I quickly suppressed them. "How was…" I swallowed. "The surgery?"

Her smile went from lovely to stunning. "It was amazing. Dr. Fredricks let me pull your appendix out."

I smiled back. That did sound cool.

"You should have seen it. Classic inflammation. Your leucocytes were elevated according to pathology. Dr. Fredricks believes it was close to rupture." *Yikes.* "I even got a chance to stitch you up. The incision over your belly button is mine."

I smiled, but the expression slowly dropped from my face. I felt exhausted.

"Get some rest. See you tomorrow," Olivia said, giving me a kiss on the cheek. I shut my eyes and smiled softly, admitting that Olivia would make an excellent doctor. Her off-duty personality was tetchy at best, but since she discovered me in pain, she had been amazing. She *was* amazing.

Chapter Nine

Olivia was there when I woke the next time. She was reading. Swallowing away the dryness of my mouth, I said, "Hey."

She looked up and smiled. "Hello."

"What you reading?"

"A paper on autoimmunity."

Just hearing her say that at this early hour hurt my brain. "Why?"

"Because, we'll be studying it soon, and you've slept half the day away."

I scrunched my forehead into a frown and tried to sit up. It hurt. "It's not breakfast time?"

She shook her head as she put her paper down to assist me. Putting some pillows behind my back, she said, "They just delivered your lunch." She pointed to a tray beside me.

The sight of food made my stomach curdle. Ignoring the tray, I looked at Olivia. "You stayed?"

Olivia shrugged her narrow shoulders. "I can read anywhere. Besides, I've been monitoring you for complications."

In other words, she was waiting to see if I'd require further surgery and score another chance to assist. "Of course you were."

"I was asked to tell you your best friend is on her way."

"Taylor's coming here?"

"Apparently. I rang your mother this morning to tell her how you were, and she said Taylor had already caught a flight to Boston."

"The charade is over, you know that right? You don't have to be here." I'm not sure why that disappointed me, especially after last night's little black dress show that we were still yet to talk about.

"I figured that had you had complications, it would be valuable experience. *That's* why I'm here. However, you seem to be recovering well."

"Sorry."

Olivia shrugged and pushed the tray closer to me. "You really should eat something."

I eyed the platter of food and no matter how I cocked my head and squinted, I couldn't figure out what the green stuff was. "What is it?"

Olivia frowned at the green goop in the bowl. "Live culture?"

I grimaced and pushed it away. "Don't suppose you could get me a sandwich from the cafeteria?"

"No, I don't suppose I could. I'm here to observe, not be your personal slave."

"My girlfriend would get me a sandwich."

"I'm not your girlfriend." Olivia smirked at me.

"You were for a little while. Doesn't that count?"

"No. I would have broken up with you by now anyway. You're high maintenance."

"Oh. Wait. *I'm* high maintenance."

Olivia remained silent, but she was still smirking.

"You're right. You didn't even let me have a New Year's kiss. I think we would have broken up before school went back and we'd be bickering like scorned lovers."

"I think saving your life counts for something. I suspect we'd at least get back to friends."

"Saving my life?" *Wait. Friends? Were we even that?*

"You were hardly in any condition to call nine-one-one."

I crossed my arms carefully. "I thought I had wind."

Olivia shook her head, then cocked it as she looked like she was listening to something in the hall. "Do you still want your New Year's kiss?" she asked me a moment later, successfully stealing the breath from my lungs.

"Uh—" Olivia didn't wait for my answer and pressed her lips against mine. It was chaste, and I was certain my mouth tasted rank having not had an opportunity to brush my teeth. It didn't seem to bother Olivia, because her lips lingered on mine, softening as she parted hers to capture my mouth with a warm, open-mouthed kiss. Damn, she was electric and there was no denying what I felt for her. Confusion be damned, I was crushing on this woman so damn hard I'm surprised I hadn't collapsed under the weight of my own heart.

Olivia pulled away and I frowned, trying to chase her lips with mine and managing to pull my stomach in the process. "Ow."

Olivia smirked at me and patted my leg, and without looking away, she said, "Hello, Taylor. Kara."

"What?" I leaned slightly to the left and saw my friend at the doorway looking awkward and confused. Beside her, Kara arrived. "Taylor?"

"Darcy, are you okay?" she said, rushing into the room at the sound of her name. She scooped me into a hug that hurt my stomach again.

"Why are you here?" I asked into the hug.

"I heard that you had to have surgery so I flew here to make sure you're okay."

Kara had swiftly followed and bodily moved Olivia to hug me and take my hand once Taylor was done with me.

"Ow."

"Gentle with the patient," Olivia snapped. "Her incisions are still tender."

"Sorry." Taylor back off, looking awkward again. Kara didn't let go of my hand.

"Hi," I said to Kara.

I noticed Taylor's frown. "Darcy?"

"Umm…Taylor, this is Kara, a friend from med school."

"Hi. I'm the best friend." She held her hand out to shake, which meant Kara had to let go of mine. *Hurray.*

"I'm Kara, the…" she looked at me. "Hopeful girlfriend?"

"What?" Taylor said with a gasp. "Darcy?" It was at this point I realized I had yet to bring Kara up in conversation with Taylor. I was turning into the worst best friend in history.

"But..." Taylor looked over at Olivia, who was smirking again.

"I'll go find out about discharging you," Olivia said, abandoning me.

"What's going on?"

"Well...I had stomach pains last night," I said. "Olivia checked on me and called the paramedics. She even got to operate on me."

"Your *girlfriend* operated on you?"

What the hell did Taylor say that for!

"Girlfriend?" Kara said abruptly. "What? But you said she was just your roommate."

"She is my roommate...umm...too?" I grimaced, this wasn't going to end well.

"So you played me?"

"No, I swear, I didn't." I looked at Taylor for backup and she raised an eyebrow at me and was that a smirk. *Damn.* I was being punished.

"Darcy? Care to explain?" Taylor asked, looking between the pair of us like we were at a tennis match.

Kara answered for me. "Your *friend* here played me. She flirted with me then agreed to go on a date with me before the *girlfriend* showed up in a skin-tight dress. Is this some kind of freaky sex game to you pair? Lure a woman in and then use her to get yourself off?"

"What! No! It wasn't anything like that at all. Olivia and I are just friends, I promise." I looked at Taylor. "Umm..."

"She's not your girlfriend then?" Taylor's eyes sparkled. She looked like she was enjoying this. "So that little lip-lock before was just platonic?"

I glanced at Kara's reddening face. "No...I..." I shut my eyes and wished the nightmare would go away.

"We were on a break," Olivia provided, making me snap my eyes back open. "Darcy was single when she accepted your date."

"I see," Kara said, clearly not convinced. "And now?"

Olivia looked at me. "That's up to Darcy."

*Oh, wonderful. Put the pressure back on m*e. Three sets of eyes stared at me waiting for my answer. Taylor smirked, Olivia raised an eyebrow, and Kara looked deadly. I licked my drying lips and kept my focus on Olivia. "I…" I took a deep breath. "I want to be your girlfriend?"

"Convincing, Darce," Taylor whispered.

"You want to date me?" Olivia asked.

I nodded tentatively back at her. "Yes?"

"And if I don't want you back?"

I hadn't thought of that and my expression fell. That was a very good question. "Then…umm…I continue being an annoying housemate."

"I hardly think you could stop being annoying if you tried."

"Says you. You're the most stubborn, controlling, intense woman I've ever met. Being neurotic is your super talent."

"Ah…Darce, I don't think that's helping your cause." Taylor said in soft warning to me.

"Listen to your friend, Darcy," Olivia said, crossing her arms. That's when I noticed the sandwich in her hand.

I grinned. "You bought me food."

"So?"

"It's something a girlfriend would do."

"Your point?"

"You're my girlfriend if you like it or not."

"Hardly, I could just be a conscientious roommate."

"*Or*, you totally love me," I blurted out as if stating fact, making Olivia straighten defensively. I beamed at her and froze when something flashed in her blue eyes and she eyed me warily. Our conversation about unrequited loves flashed through my mind. The way she looked like she wanted to tear Kara's throat out. The way she looked after me by making sure

I ate right, by telling me to get enough sleep, and by washing my clothes. Yes, she said it was cheaper and more efficient, but really, it was a really nice thing to do for someone you *tolerated*. "Oh, my God," I said equally as blurt-like. Smooth operator.

Olivia let out a rush of breath. I had no idea what Taylor or Kara were doing at that moment because all I could see was Olivia standing at the foot of the bed looking vulnerable and ready to sprint in the other direction.

I stared at her and said, "No way."

She shrugged a shoulder and looked a little broken.

"But…"

"Ugh. I've had enough. Have a nice life," Kara said, storming out leaving the room awkwardly quiet.

"You like me?" I asked Olivia, not daring to use the other 'L' word. It was too big. She didn't answer me and continued staring at me as if I should have all the answers. Good luck. I wet my drying lips as the thought of her kiss and all that hand-holding in the last twenty-four hours sprang to mind. "Same."

She smiled at me in a weird conceited, all-knowing way. "I know."

She what? How could she know? Hell, I didn't even know until just then. What gave her the right to get ahead of me? I was so confused.

Taylor broke the silence when she poked around at the green goop on my food tray. "What is that?"

"No idea."

She pushed it away and sighed. "So…Olivia operated on you?"

"I know. Cool, right? Our professor was my surgeon and he asked her to assist."

"Isn't that like some ethical problem?" Taylor asked, looking between us.

Olivia approached the unoccupied side of the bed and shrugged her shoulders. "Not really. To him, we're just students."

"He doesn't know you're dating? Or pretend dating. Or whatever it is you're doing now?"

"Not really," I said.

"Why not?"

"It never came up."

We were silent for a moment. Olivia passed me the sandwich and I sneered at it. Wholemeal bread with what looked like too much green stuff between it. "What is that?"

"A salad sandwich."

"It looks worse that whatever that is," I said, pointing at the goop in the bowl.

"It's lettuce, sprouts, and egg. It's good for you."

I grimaced.

"Fine. Give it back. Go hungry."

"No." I clutched the clear plastic container to my chest and my stomach growled.

Olivia shook her head at me and excused herself to get the discharge papers the nurse said she'd have ready for her.

"Do you two have anything in common?"

"I guess so." Participating in fraudulent relationships came to mind.

"Would you mind if I stayed with you while I'm here?"

"I don't mind at all. I'm sure Olivia won't either."

"Won't mind what?" Olivia asked, returning with a form.

"If I stay with you while I'm in town?" Taylor said.

Olivia shrugged. "That's fine. You can have the spare room."

Spare room? What spare room? "Huh?"

"You're with me so I can continue to monitor you," Olivia said. Taylor sniggered and earned herself a glare. "For complications," she added.

Taylor kept sniggering anyway.

Olivia left Taylor and I alone after that. She told us she needed to collect groceries and do a load of washing. Knowing she shopped yesterday and did her laundry then, I assumed she was readying the apartment to give Taylor the *spare room*. When I was released from the hospital that evening, I was proved right.

Olivia, who had wrapped her arm around my waist and left it there since leaving my hospital bed, guided me into her room. I discovered a great deal of my personal items in the room, and some of my clothes crammed into the closet. Would it continue to look like this when Taylor returned home?

Olivia settled me into the double bed and kissed my forehead.

"Thank you," I whispered.

Olivia smiled. She had done that a lot this past twenty-four hours. "You're welcome."

Taylor, who had been hovering in the doorway, left. Since we left the hospital, she'd become a little weird and quiet. "Is it just me, or does Taylor look, I don't know, bothered or something?"

Olivia's smile abruptly vanished and she walked out of the room without a word.

"Was it something I said?"

8∽

It took another day before I was able to get out of bed and gingerly walk around. Olivia had cited an overload of studying she needed to do at the library and had left Taylor and I alone for a considerable part of the day. She had even slept on the couch the night before. Where I once craved the company of Taylor, I couldn't help but feel a little antsy that Olivia had abandoned me during my recovery. I mean, aren't we supposed to be together now? For real. I was confused.

"Why didn't you tell me about Kara?"

"Umm…" I shrugged, not knowing how to answer that. Taylor huffed and took her dinner plate to the kitchen. It dawned on me that that must be why she seemed so snippy. We told each other everything, with the exception of her sleeping with Charli, so me not telling her something big about having a girlfriend, twice, must have been gnawing at her. "I'm sorry," I said when she returned and fell onto the sofa beside me.

"For what?"

"Not telling you about Kara."

Taylor sniffed and shifted in her chair. "Yeah...well...I figured it was something you should have mentioned."

"I know." Sighing, I said, "I was...clueless. I don't know how this dating stuff works. Olivia said she's been flirting with me all year, but honestly, I had no idea."

"Olivia said so?"

I scratched my head before nodding. "Yeah. Kara has been interested since New Year, and Olivia noticed."

"And you didn't think to tell me about this woman?"

"Umm..."

Taylor huffed. "I could have helped you figure it out. I mean, that's what *best friends* are for, isn't it?"

"Yes?"

"Exactly. I feel like I barely know you at the moment. You have women flirting with you, Olivia looking after you, and me, well, I have no idea what my role is anymore."

I knitted my eyebrows together. Taylor thought I had superseded her with Olivia? This was why she was snippy? I let out a breath of relief. She was jealous again, but for an entirely different reason. "I love you."

She pursed her lips and sniffed.

"I've known you since birth. You know all my secrets. You're my best friend and you're important to my life. Without you, I wouldn't be here. I wouldn't have met Olivia, who, by the way, is pissed off at me for reasons I don't understand."

"What do you mean, pissed off?"

I shrugged and winced as the movement made my stomach pull. "I said you looked bothered last night and she up and stormed off. What's that about?"

Taylor narrowed her eyes. "Bothered?"

"Yeah. You looked kinda jealous, I guess."

"And you said that to Olivia after just having some weird conversation about dating each other? And, not to mention, after your ridiculous pretend relationship designed to make me jealous?"

"Umm."

Taylor shook her head and started to laugh at me. "For someone that's never been in a relationship before, you do a stunning job of making it look like a soap opera."

I grimaced. "Thank you."

"Idiot."

I pouted at that.

"You can figure your relationship problems out all on your own."

My face fell.

Taylor relaxed into the chair and said, "For what it's worth, I think you two make a good if odd, couple. I'm happy for you. I hope you realize what you've got there and stop crushing on other people, or pretending to crush on other people."

"Yeah, me too."

Taylor leaned over and kissed my cheek. "I'm going to go wash up."

"Okay." Leaning back into the sofa, I woke up there several hours later with a groan. I hadn't meant to fall asleep.

"You're awake."

I blinked and twisted my head. Olivia was sitting at her desk. "Hi. I didn't hear you come in."

"You were snoring, so I'm not surprised."

Gingerly, I sat up. "Where's Taylor?"

"Bed," Olivia said with a huff.

"What time is it?"

"Midnight."

I frowned and stood from the sofa. "Why are you still up?"

Olivia shrugged. "You were sleeping in my spot."

"Your spot?" She didn't answer. Shuffling over, I put a hand on her shoulder. "Come on. Let's go to bed."

"Go ahead."

"No, you're coming, too."

Olivia stood and confronted me with a hiss. "Why? So we can make Taylor jealous in the morning? Are we leaving the door open so she can see us spooning?"

"What? No."

Olivia bared her teeth at me making me wonder what the hell I'd done wrong this time. I racked my brain for ideas and came up empty. Grabbing her by the elbow, I shuffled us to the bedroom and shut the door.

"What's wrong with you?" I asked.

"I'm tired of being a pawn in your twisted little game."

"A pawn in what game?"

"I think you missed your calling, your acting skills back at the hospital were phenomenal. An Oscar-winning performance."

"Performance? I wasn't performing."

Olivia crossed her arms and glared at me. "So your comment about how Taylor looked *bothered* when we returned to the apartment was what? You *not* trying to win her affections again?"

"What?" I played the moment over again as well as the conversation with Taylor. I gasped. Taylor was right, I'm an idiot. "No. Taylor and I are friends. She was pissed I hadn't told her about your *best buddy*, Kara, and she thought I was replacing her. I wasn't lying at the hospital. I want to be your girlfriend." A shiver of excitement ran through me at stating those words so boldly. Sighing, I said on the outgoing air, "I really like you. I think." Olivia rolled her eyes so I scowled at her. "I don't really know what it is I feel, but it's new, it's scary, and kind of exciting."

Olivia narrowed her eyes at me before relaxing her posture. "So this is real?"

I nodded.

"Huh," she said, contemplating the notion.

"Do you..." I swallowed, suddenly unsure. "Still like me back? Or something?"

Olivia huffed. "Against my better judgment, yes."

I grinned.

"Don't look so smug."

I scoffed a little too hard and put my hand protectively over my incisions. "Says you. You looked like the cat that got the cream in the bar that night. Damn, that dress…" I trailed off shaking my head.

"I was simply trying to prove a point."

"What point?"

"This one," she said, cradling my cheeks gently and pulling me in for a kiss. Sighing as our mouths touched, she imparted gentle kisses on my lips.

"That's a good point," I said quietly as she pulled away to rest her forehead against mine.

She laughed softly and shook her head against mine. "This is such a bad idea."

So true.

Chapter Ten

I had a medical note that excused me from Monday's classes, and Taylor and I spent the day wisely. We had a Sandra Bullock movie marathon. I should have been studying, considering I'd lost my weekend to hospital and bedroom confinement, but since Taylor was leaving the next the morning, I figured Olivia would make me catch up.

I smiled. Since sharing that kiss last night, I'd felt giddy. I woke to Olivia bustling about the room getting ready for school. I was saddened to miss how she woke. Did we cuddle? Did she drool in her sleep? Did she snore? *Hell.* Did *I* snore?

"What are you panicking about?" Olivia asked, pausing in her clothes gathering task when she noticed I was awake.

"Snoring. Did I?"

Olivia smiled. "No, you didn't."

I sighed a breath of relief.

"You do fidget a lot."

"You try and get comfortable sleeping on your back. I prefer my side."

"I prefer my back."

I smiled. That meant I got to cuddle up against her, head resting on her shoulder, arm wrapped around her waist, her neck *just there* to kiss. I stopped my internal rambling and tried to look innocent.

"Now what?" Olivia asked, narrowing her eyes at me suspiciously.

"Nothing."

"Hmm."

Deciding against interrogating me, she got ready for school with practiced efficiency and left, leaving me to lay in for a little longer.

"On a scale of one to ten, how attractive do you think she is?" Taylor asked me through a mouthful of popcorn deep into *The Proposal*.

I looked at Sandra Bullock and bit my lip. "Eight. You?"

"Nine and a half."

"What about Betty White?"

"Oh, definitely a ten. Anyone that looks that good at that age earns top points in my book."

Taylor nodded. "True. And Olivia?"

"Eleven."

Taylor chuckled. "You've got it bad, haven't you?"

I sighed. "Very."

Just how bad I had it for Olivia proved itself after Taylor left the next day. After waving her off at the bus stop, Olivia and I walked to school together. She had decided to chaperone my recovering body to school just in case. Knowing she had taken time out of her precise schedule to escort me made my stomach feel gooey and warm. It was the first time we had walked together to classes. Olivia liked to arrive fifteen minutes before classes started, and I often ran in at the last minute. I couldn't stop smiling that she was beside me, or wondering whether I should hold her hand or not.

"What is it?" Olivia asked me after we crossed the busiest road between us and Harvard Medical.

"What is what?"

"You keep looking at me strangely. It's making me uncomfortable."

"Oh. Sorry." My happy bubble popped and I shifted away from her a little.

"Are you feeling okay?"

"Yeah. I'm fine. More than fine, actually." I scratched at my neck.

Olivia stopped and raised an eyebrow at me. "Then what's making you act stranger than usual?"

I shifted my bag on my shoulder and shrugged casually. "I'm not strange."

"Hmm," Olivia said after a moment before she continued walking.

I stopped looking at her hand and wondering how warm it would feel in mine, and instead watched the world go by. A few minutes later, we walked into the auditorium and I followed Olivia to her seat.

"What are you doing?" she asked me with a frown as I sat beside her.

"Umm…getting ready for the lecture?"

"I prefer to sit alone."

"Seriously?" *What happened to the like stuff and the girlfriend agreement?*

Olivia gave me a smile and took my hand, giving it a squeeze. "I'm sorry, but you distract me."

"Oh." I put my best wounded puppy look on my face.

"Nice try," she said, shaking her head at me. "Now scoot. Dr. Deakins is about to start."

Pouting and muttering under my breath, I moved out of her row and went to my usual chair. Kara glared at me as I passed her. I gave her a little finger wave. There was nothing wrong with being friendly, was there? Kara relaxed and shot me a tight-lipped smile. I noticed Olivia's stern look before I sat in my seat. I blew her a kiss before tuning in on Dr. Deakins' presentation on cellular, molecular and biochemical processes in the respiratory system. The morning flew past in a flurry of case studies and discussions.

§

"Lunch?" I asked Olivia as I caught her hurrying from the auditorium later.

"Sorry. Can't." She checked her watch and extended her stride.

"Where are you going?" I said, jogging after her and wincing as the movement tore at my surgery wounds.

"A seminar on natural antibodies on inflammatory and autoimmune diseases at the Forsyth Institute."

"But that's across the river."

"Which is why I need to hurry. The bus leaves in a minute. Do you want to come?"

I nodded.

"Right." Olivia began a jog, which I thought was highly unfair. There was no way I could keep up. I settled for striding along behind her with my much shorter legs. She reached the bus, one foot on the step, and talked to the bus driver before smiling back at me. "Come on, slow poke."

"You try running with three holes in your belly," I grumbled as I stepped past her into the bus.

When Olivia sat beside me, my efforts were rewarded as she took my hand and kissed my cheek. Transported back into the giddy girl with a hopeless infatuation, I followed Olivia around for the remainder of the day like a lost puppy. I was pathetic.

I was also a little lost that night.

With Taylor gone, I no longer had an excuse to sleep in Olivia's bed, but that didn't stop me from continuing my puppy-dog routine and standing beside what had become *my* side of the bed, staring down at it hopefully. Olivia was currently showering, and having dressed in her room considering all my clothes were still in there, I was uncertain about what to do next. Am I allowed to just climb in? Would Olivia march me out? I had no idea, and with no previous relationship experience to fall back on, I sighed and started to shuffle from the room.

"Where are you going?" Olivia asked when she eyed me and my pillow walking past the bathroom door she just opened.

"Bed?"

"We haven't changed the sheets."

About to argue that Taylor was hardly going to dirty them inside two days, I clamped my lips shut. "You're right. So…umm…I'm sleeping in your bed again?"

Olivia smirked at me. "There is the couch."

Damn. I nodded and made my way to the lounge.

"Wait." Olivia hooked her arm around my elbow. "I was kidding. You're welcome to share my bed."

"Oh. Cool. Thanks."

I lay on her bed like a board. Stiff, unmoving and I think I stopped breathing just in case I snored. The past few nights, sleeping in Olivia's bed was easier. She had waited until I fell asleep before climbing in beside me, so I didn't have to go through the torture of bed etiquette of a newly established relationship. And really, what was the relationship anyway but a couple of kisses, a few stitches in my stomach and some hand holding. Back in my bed in Minnesota, I was too busy plotting ways to get Taylor to fall for me to worry about the woman lying in the dark beside me. Now I was as nervous as a wild rabbit. *Wait…were wild rabbit's even nervous creatures? Maybe a squirrel would be a better analogy?* I hummed to myself.

"Darcy?"

"Hmm?"

"Why are you muttering about squirrels?"

Oh, crap. I'm about to sound crazy. "Umm…they're nervous creatures, aren't they?"

Olivia turned her head to look at me. I could just make out her form in the darkened room. "Not as nervous as you."

"Hey. I'm not nervous."

"Then why are you hugging the edge of the bed and trying your best to impersonate a log?"

"Umm…" Olivia shifted onto her side as I continued staring at the ceiling. I yelped and slapped at whatever touched my cheek. I ended up slapping Olivia's hand. I could feel the bed moving with her silent chuckles as my heart rate tried to slow. "That's unfair. I thought you were a spider or something."

"Darcy?"

"Yes."

"Breathe."

I took a deep breath and heaved it out. "Now what?"

Olivia found one of my hands where it was currently pressed against my sternum. "Relax."

I nodded and continued to take deep breaths, concentrating on the way her thumb caressed my knuckles. It was really nice and also really new. Smiling, I enjoyed the sensation and let my eyes drift closed.

∽

Moaning against the intrusion of sunlight on my eyelids, I burrowed into the warmth around me. An alarm rudely went off a few minutes later, forcing me to squeeze my eyes shut and hug the warm thing I was tucked up against as it moved. A second later, the irritating noise stopped.

"Morning," said Olivia. Her amused-sounding voice rumble below my ear. Odd.

I forced my eyelids up and saw an expanse of skin in front of me. I found myself staring at Olivia's clavicle. Shifting my head, I spotted her neck, chin, and then smiling mouth. "Morning."

"I see my squirrel found her bravery last night."

I poked my tongue out at her and she laughed, jostling my head in the process.

"Come on my cute little rodent, time to get up."

"I'm not a rodent," I mumbled as I burrowed under the covers, trying to recover the warmth she had just let escape.

"But you are cute," she said. I quickly shoved the covers down to find myself alone. It didn't stop me from grinning. Olivia had just called me cute.

"You think I'm cute?" I asked her over my morning coffee fifteen minutes later.

"You have your moments," she said as she scooped her egg-white-only omelet from the pan.

"How many moments?"

"You've had one so far."

I pouted.

"Careful, the wind might change and your face will be stuck looking like a sulking toddler."

"I'm not sulking."

Olivia smiled and pushed a plate of freshly made omelet at me. "Happy Valentine's Day."

"It's Valentine's Day? Since when?" *How had I missed this rather significant date on the calendar?* I rubbed at the stitches rubbing against my jean waistline. Damn appendix.

"Since 496 AD."

Ugh. Trust Olivia to know a random fact like that.

"Eat up," she said, walking around the counter and kissing me on the cheek. "See you at school."

"Wait. You're leaving without me?"

Olivia paused and frowned. "You want me to wait?" She looked at her watch and I saw her eye twitch.

"No. It's fine. You go on ahead."

Olivia nodded and opened the front door.

"Wait!"

"Yes?"

"Thank you." I held up my breakfast.

"You're welcome."

She left and I stared down at my very wholesome breakfast. Usually grabbing a piece of toast or just surviving on coffee alone, I smiled and dove into the meal. Olivia was the best. It was then I concluded that she hadn't eaten anything but an apple. I looked at my plate with suspicion. I had a sneaky feeling she made this for herself but ran out of time to eat it. Shrugging, I decided I didn't care.

❧

I spent the day plotting, and for once, I wasn't plotting Olivia's demise. Yes, she was still irritating and difficult, but now she was my girlfriend, so I was obliged to do something for Valentine's. I ruled out flowers remembering the disaster of bringing in a bouquet of daisies once and inciting a severe allergic reaction in my roommate. I had wanted to brighten up my desk space and provide inspiration for my study. Fail.

I thought of chocolates when I opened the Reese's bar I had brought along with me for lunch, then remembered every single lecture Olivia had given me about empty calories and blood sugar spikes and long term fat storage, not to mention her freak status at not liking chocolate in the first place. Subtly poking at my stomach, I reminded myself I should go for a run as soon as I was able.

I munched on my treat and sighed. What does someone get a person like Olivia to show them they care?

Screwing up the empty foil packet of my chocolate, I threw it in the bin on the way to my next class. I stopped as soon as my eyes caught the notice board and the schedule for upcoming seminars. *Perfect!*

෨

"Hi," I said, coming up behind Olivia on her walk home. She screeched and swatted me with her bag.

"Hey."

"Darcy?" She clamped a hand over her chest. "What the hell are you trying to do?"

I grimaced. "Sorry."

"God." Olivia took a deep breath and shook her head at me.

"I needed to catch you."

"What for?"

"Umm…I want to ask you out on a date."

Her eyes turned wary and she slowly shook her head. "I don't think that's a good idea."

Wait. What? Weren't we technically dating? "But—"

"Look, Darcy, I know we're doing this girlfriend thing for real now, but you need to know that I don't date. Ever."

"But…*seriously?*"

"Seriously."

I folded my arms across my chest and glared. I had never been in a relationship before, and I had no intentions of missing out on the awkward dating scene. I needed the experience. "Well, too bad."

"Excuse me."

"We're going on a date tonight because it's Valentine's and you're my girlfriend and it's the right thing to do."

"No."

"Yes."

"Darcy—"

I held up my hand and fished around in my bag for a moment. "Here." I shoved a bouquet of pencils at her. "Flowers."

"They're HB pencils."

"Because you're allergic to flowers."

"Only daisies."

"Oh…well…this is more useful."

Olivia looked at the mug full of pencils in her hand and smiled. "Actually, it is."

"Exactly. And now, you're coming with me because you feel indebted. Come on." I grabbed her free hand and tugged her along. She reluctantly walked behind me.

"You should know, I don't feel the slightest bit indebted to you for these pencils. I did make you omelets this morning."

"Omelets that you ran out of time to eat."

I smirked when Olivia's eyes widened and she stopped walking. "How—"

"Did I know? Because you have some sort of protein every single morning. Except today." I stepped closer to her. "You gave me second-hand omelets."

"There's no such thing as second-hand food. I hardly regurgitated it."

"Ew. Nice visual."

"You're welcome."

I took Olivia's hand again and walked us along. "The point is, you owe me now. I got you an *actual* gift and not a plate of leftovers. And now I'm going to collect."

Olivia sighed. "Fine. Where are we going then?"

"Well, we have to hurry to get some food, then get over to the children's hospital."

"What?"

I smiled. "You'll see."

A couple of containers of sushi later, and I walked Olivia into the Folkman Auditorium at the children's hospital for a lecture on cell biology.

"This is your idea of a date?" Olivia said, at the auditorium door, yanking on my hand and forcing me to stop.

I had a nasty feeling I'd made a wrong move. "Umm...yes?"

She looked at me blankly for a moment before tugging me to the women's toilets. I prepared myself for a defense testimony which I launched into the moment we checked the bathroom was unoccupied. "I'm sorry! I thought you'd like this over some try-hard romantic dinner by candlelight. I promise we can go and do something else if you like?"

Olivia's eyebrows rose. Her mouth began to turn up at the corners and soon she was smiling at me.

"Umm...so...did you want to go?" I said nervously.

"No. I don't." Olivia stepped forward and hooked me behind the neck and pulled me against her. Her lips met mine with a satisfied groan and my legs began to wobble. *Damn that sound was devastating.* My back was suddenly up against the cool tiled wall and my lips had been parted with a needy tongue. *Gosh, how this woman could kiss.* Feeling the need to give some of the feels back, I wrapped my arms around her waist and pulled her tight against me while I slid my tongue past her lips. She made an approving noise and had someone not walked in and yelped at us, I may very well have got to second base.

We parted in a flurry of panting breaths and I went bright red. Olivia began to chuckle, a sound that made my confidence inflate.

"Come on, cute squirrel, we have a seminar to attend."
Olivia thinks I'm cute.

Chapter Eleven

Olivia and I continued to share a bed despite the fact that we had no visitors and the sheets in my room were fresh and clean. I like to think it was my cuteness that kept me beside her each night. I spent a week having no idea how I was supposed to be acting around her but was pleased to see Olivia's abrupt personality didn't change. She was easier to deal with when she was being bossy and anal. I knew *that* Olivia. The one that emerged when I was in hospital, the caring, and touchy-feely one, was difficult to pinpoint. I figured all the touching would come back in time.

And bit by bit, it did.

She still went to school at the break of dawn, and I dawdled and dashed in late. Just in time to catch the start of the class and take my seat near, but not beside her. After classes, she'd wait for me citing that she was catching up on reading or research while I lingered talking to fellow students, and we walked home together. This was the moment of the day I enjoyed the most because more often than not, she'd hold my hand. I walked home on those days grinning like a fool.

We'd prepare dinner and eat it together as we discussed the day's lessons. We'd study the rest of the night away and collapse into bed exhausted as the clock struck midnight. Monday to Friday, we'd repeat the process each day. Weekends differed…slightly. I managed to rearrange my shifts at the dry cleaner for Saturday and Sunday night. Olivia let me sleep in Saturdays before enjoying a day full of study, muted ball games, and sips of cheap beer. Sunday, I'd get a cooking lesson and then clean the house while Olivia washed the clothes. After that…more study. There wasn't a lot of time outside of that rigorous schedule for kissing, touching, and nakedness. Medicine had taken over my life.

Class schedules changed again, and we undertook more exams and assessment tasks and suddenly, we had three classes left until we'd completed year one of our medical training. One night, Olivia had been snappier than usual as she read through her notes from our first Immunology, Microbiology, and Pathology lecture. She kept rubbing at her neck as I prepared dinner which was an advanced version of pasta that she had taught me the week previous.

"You okay?" I called out as I closed the oven on the lasagna.

"What?" she muttered.

"I said, are you okay?" I walked over to her and put a hand on her back. She swatted at it immediately. "Hey." I raised my hands in defense.

She looked instantly guilty and slumped over with a sigh. "Sorry."

I tentatively returned my hand to her back and rubbed slow circles. "What's up?"

Rubbing her eyes, she said, "Nothing. Tired I guess."

I nodded and stepped in behind her and started kneading at the muscles of her shoulders. The moan she let out did funny things to my tummy. I kept massaging her tense shoulders and dropped a kiss on her hair. "We've been working hard this past month or so, why don't we forget about medicine and go and do something different for a couple of days?"

As expected, Olivia shook her head. I don't think the woman knew what relaxation or fun looked like. I pushed my thumbs in deeper and elicited another moan from her that made me smile. It was nice to do this. I spent most of my time looking at her and hoping I wasn't being too obvious. I memorized the way the planes of her neck met her shoulder, and how the warming weather meant I could spend many long minutes or hours dreaming about touching the creamy skin that dropped from her throat to the swell of her breasts. More often than not, I was caught in those moments and spent a good deal of time blushing.

Each morning I woke up wrapped around her like a boa constrictor. She never complained, and I cherished the times I woke before her so I could linger in the moment and enjoy the soft flesh beneath my cheek, arm and leg that was inevitably curled around her. Apart from holding hands, touching wasn't a regular thing outside of the bedroom.

Kissing was even more irregular. Sometimes, she'd surprise me and I'd suddenly be backed up against something having the breath kissed from my lungs. I never had the nerve to initiate those moments, so I relied solely on her mood to feel her lips below mine. I'd often thought I should woman-up and make a move. Perhaps that's what she was waiting for and her frustration burst out in random acts of passion.

Those passionate moments always ended the same. She'd grunt and push herself off me before vacating the scene entirely. It left me feeling ravaged but confused. My dreams would become vivid after days like those. Thankfully, the weather was still cool enough for her to wear a high-necked top that day.

"Liv," I said softly into her hair as I left my mouth pressed against her head.

"It's Olivia."

"Mmm. Will you come away with me this weekend?"

She leaned forward and looked up at me, breaking the contact I had with her hair and shoulders. "We have exams coming up in a few weeks."

"And spring recess starts Monday. Please. Just for a couple of days."

"A couple of days that we could spent preparing for the integration exercise."

I heaved out a breath and stepped back a few inches. "Yeah. You're right." Nodding and feeling utterly demoralized, I turned to walk away but found she had snagged my hand.

"I'm sorry."

I didn't look back at her. "It's fine." Gathering my running clothes, I swiftly changed and headed to the door.

"Where do you think you're going?" Olivia asked as she glared at me from her desk.

"For a run."

She shook her head. "No. Your incisions—"

"Are fine." I opened the door and shut it before she had a chance to say anything further. I knew I was running away, but I had no idea what it was I needed to do to take the tentative relationship I had with Olivia to that next rung. Tension burned nervously in me every time I was around her, and knowing that her education was more important than me, despite her declaration of love, was a little disheartening. I had selfishly hoped that our feelings would rise and conquer all and that I'd at least have experienced an orgasm by now. Sharing a bed made releasing sexual tension at my own hands a little awkward, and being unable to get out and run had added to my frustration.

Limbering up at the front of our apartment block, I took a deep breath and jogged a few steps, grimacing against the tug of pain at my suture sites. Perhaps this wasn't a good idea after all. Slowing to a pace that didn't hurt, I walked and walked and walked. My plan to exercise my frustrations away didn't work, and I found myself thinking about Olivia with a renewed intensity. The woman was a walking conflict. Passionate, but distant. Confident, but sometimes, so unsure, especially when it came to me apparently.

I sighed. Maybe it was time I grew a backbone and made a move. Yes, I had zero experience with this relationship business, but that didn't mean I shouldn't start trying. I wanted to touch her so badly my fingers ached constantly. I wanted to kiss her obsessively, and I wanted to take her away from the medicinal world and focus on her without distraction. Spring break meant a week with no classes. A week of opportunity to woo my girlfriend.

My mind preoccupied with all things Olivia, I didn't realize I'd followed Columbus Avenue all the way to downtown

Boston until the street ran out and I was practically standing in the Boston Common gardens.

"Huh," I said with a grunt as I stared at the parklands in front of me. Shrugging and figuring I'd not really explored Boston enough, I crossed the road and wandered about the common. It was full of budding plants, busy with activity from tai chi groups to people running with Frisbees, and the bridge over the water attracted a bevy of lovers judging from a number of people kissing. Watching them depressed me. I should be on that bridge with Olivia. We should be the couple lounging under that tree on the picnic rug laying back and reading. We should be the ones riding those horses.

I shook my head. *No.* I don't do horses.

Despite that, I bit my lip and stared at the scenes around me. Perhaps if I couldn't convince Olivia to spend time away, I could encourage her to spend a day with me here just lolling about relaxing. Plan forming, I smiled and headed back to the apartment.

80

"Morning," I said, snuggling into Olivia's side as I roused on the first day of spring break.

"Morning," she said in return as she tried to climb from the bed.

I tightened my arm around her and shook my head. "No. You're staying here."

"Pardon?"

I leaned up on my elbow and smiled at her. "I have plans for you today, and that starts with you staying here."

Olivia frowned at me, suspicion all over her expression. "Plans?"

I nodded.

She narrowed her eyes. "And what if I had something arranged already? Did you think of that?"

My mood sagged. "Oh." I bit the inside of my cheek for a moment. "Do you?"

"Have plans?"

"Mmm."

"Beyond reading journal articles, no."

Big sigh of relief. "Good. Then stay put." I threw myself out of bed and shut the door, catching her amused look as I left.

Operation Romancing Olivia, initiated.

I rattled about the kitchen making breakfast and soon wandered back into the room expecting to find her lying in bed.

"Hey," I said, protesting to find her up and dressed and perched at the end of the neatly made bed. She'd even brushed her dark hair and pulled it into a ponytail that draped down her back.

Olivia looked at the tray of food I carried. "You didn't specify that I was supposed to remain in bed." She looked back up at me. "Eating in the place you sleep isn't exactly sanitary."

I sighed. "Fine." I turned and headed back to the kitchen, depositing her omelet, coffee and plastic flower on the counter. "I made you breakfast in bed. Sort of."

Olivia, for her part, at least looked a little ashamed. "Thank you. What's the occasion?"

"Us."

"Us?"

"Yes. Now eat up while I change."

Thirty minutes later, and with a significantly heavy backpack hanging from my shoulders, Olivia and I walked into Boston.

"Where are we going? Is there a seminar on?"

"We're having a day off. No study. No medicine. Just you and me."

Her hand began to sweat a few minutes later and I was forced to let it go so I could dry my hand. "You okay?" I asked as we neared Boston Common.

"Mmm."

Convincing. "So," I said as we entered the Common. "This is my plan." I swept my arm across the horizon full of people milling around the park in various stages of fun and relaxation.

"I don't understand."

I shook my head and reached for her hand. "Come on, I'll show you."

Deep into the park, I aimed for the tree I scoped out last week. Pulling a blanket from my backpack, I spread it on the grass and gestured for her to sit.

"We're having a picnic?" she asked.

"Of sorts."

She arched an eyebrow at me then looked dubiously at the rug. I sat down and organized the contents of my bag. Thermos of coffee. A couple of containers of food. Water. Sunblock, and hats.

Olivia sat beside me and sighed.

"Have you ever been on a picnic before?" I asked.

"No."

"Not even as a kid?"

"Not even then."

That was mildly depressing. "Well then, welcome to your inaugural picnic. I'll be your hostess for the day, and I promise fun, food and fresh air."

Olivia gave me a frown. "Why?"

"Why what?"

"Why are we doing this? I have things to—"

I reached over and took her hand and gave it a sharp squeeze. "Stop. Stop thinking about school just for a few hours. All the things you have to do will be there when we get home. So, do me a favor and just...I don't know...relax? Do you know how to do that?"

Olivia's eyes narrowed. "No."

I sighed and let my thumb skim the back of her soft hands. "Then let me help you, okay? Please. For me?"

She rolled her shoulders and sat up straighter as she contemplated my query. Taking a deep breath, she looked across the park and studied the other park-goers. After a long exhale, she said quietly, "Fine."

That felt like an overwhelming victory to me, so with a broad grin on my face, I guided her through the picnicking etiquette. Eat as much as you can, wash it all down with a beverage, then laze about staring at the clouds.

We were staring at the fluffy white shapes in the sky an hour later when she said, "So how long are we doing this for?"

"The picnic? For the rest of the day."

She huffed.

"Hey, you promised."

"I didn't promise, I said I'll try."

"So, try then."

"I have." She sat up and sighed.

"Then try harder," I said, sitting up as well.

"Darcy, this kind of activity, it isn't me. I can't be idle, not when I have other things to attend to."

"Study isn't going anywhere, but your life is."

"What's that supposed to mean? You think I'm wasting my life studying a profession that's supposed to save lives?"

"No, that's not what I meant at all." Huffing out a breath and running a hand through tangled hair, I shook my head. "What I mean is that sometimes you need to live a little. Medicine will always be there for you, but this," I said, sweeping my hand across the view again. "This is what you're missing while you're cooped up at a desk. Without this perspective, without *living*, how are you supposed to understand *why* you're saving people?"

"What do you mean, why? I thought that much was obvious."

I growled as she misunderstood me again. "Liv—"

"Olivia."

"—it's these kind of experiences that you're trying to let people get back to. These kinds of memories you want the kids you'll be saving to grow up and enjoy. Do you see what I mean?

If you haven't had them, then you won't understand just how precious the gift of life really is."

She arched her eyebrows at me and a dark, scary look crossed her face. "You're trying to tell me I don't understand how precious life is?"

I shook my head with a weary sigh. *Was this woman going to constantly misunderstand me?*

Olivia stood, brushing off her jeans. "This picnic is over."

I rushed to my feet. "No. It isn't."

"I'm not going to sit here doing *nothing* while you lecture me on why my life is miserable. You have no idea where I've come from and what I've experienced, so you can take your arrogant judgments and shove them elsewhere."

"Stop." I grabbed her arm before she had a chance to escape.

She tried to yank her arm from my grip. "Let me go."

"Liv, please." My breath had shortened with fear that Olivia was going to run and I'd lost my chance with her for good. The look in her eyes was unlike anything I'd seen before. It wasn't annoyed Olivia. It wasn't caring Olivia. It was a scared one. One that looked ready to run and never stop. "Please," I said in a whisper. "I'm not judging you. I just…I…" I sighed. "I just want to make some memories with you. You know? Something that we can look back on and smile that doesn't involve classes, and study and cadavers."

She scowled at the grass at our feet.

"You're right, I know nothing about your past, and if I said something that hurt you, I promise I'm sorry and didn't mean it." I sighed and let go of her arm. If she wanted to leave, who was I to stop her? Surprising me, she stayed still. Considering that, I figured I should start telling some truths. "I don't know what I'm doing."

She looked at me. *Progress.*

"I…I don't know what it is you want. I don't know what I'm supposed to do. I think we're supposed to be dating, but I've got no idea. All we really do is share a bed. I feel like I'm

barely hanging on. I want to touch you like *all* the time, but…"
I took a deep breath. "I don't know if you want that." Rubbing
my forehead and ignoring the hot water welling in my eyes, I
looked at the rug perched in the shaded grass and said, "I
wanted to do something with you, something girlfriends would
do together, to see if I can figure it out. I'm clueless here."

After a considerable silence, Olivia said, "I've noticed."

I let out a tense chuckle and chanced a look at her. She was
staring at the red plaid blanket on the grass. "You're right," she
said. "I haven't made many memories like this. My life has
been…hard." She sucked her bottom lip into her mouth and
looked nervous and on the verge of tears. "I…" She huffed out
a breath. "I want to prove I wasn't worth tossing away."

My heart shattered. Olivia was accomplished, incredibly
clever, and should have been the apple of any parents' eye. I
wanted to wrap her up in my arms and tell her she was worth
everything, but I figured that may have been too much for her
right now. I reached out and took her hand, happy she allowed
the touch. "Sit with me," I said quietly.

She took a long breath through her nose and inclined her
head on the exhale.

We sat, and I pulled something from my backpack to hand
to her. She blinked at the sudden appearance of her notepad
and the lecture notes she had been neck-deep in yesterday. I laid
back on the rug and patted my stomach, hopefully conveying to
her that she could use me as a pillow.

"Are you sure?"

I patted my stomach again and to my eternal delight, she
picked up her notes and lay against me.

I sighed and relaxed under her gentle weight, and as I stared
at the clouds and ran my fingers through her hair, I fell asleep
as a contended girlfriend.

I woke disorientated, and with a weight draped down the
length of my body. Blinking, I turned to find Olivia had
abandoned her books and was asleep against my side. I smiled
and took in the beauty of her resting features. "So beautiful," I

whispered and pressed my lips against her temple. She stirred under my touch and blue eyes soon blinked up at me. I ran my knuckles down her cheek and emboldened by her sleepy stare, I leaned down and kissed her.

It was the first time I'd initiated this kind of intimacy and felt the rush of adrenaline flood my body. Savoring the taste and touch of her lips against mine for as long as possible, I managed to make the kiss languid and tender. This was a new dimension for us, and Olivia's response was to go boneless and pliable below me, allowing me to take the dominant stance. Confidence joined the adrenaline coursing through me, and I deepened the kiss with a moan and possessive delve of my tongue.

Olivia submitted to it and our breath shortened as the act got more and more intimate and passionate. Evening spring air touched my skin as my shirt rode up when her hand pushed below my top, and with a surge of need to repay the touch, I let my hand run up her side to fondle my first ever breast. Feeling her supple and weighty breast below my hand nearly short-circuited the rest of me. I forgot to breathe. I stopped the movements of my mouth and tongue, and I focused entirely on exploring her chest. Running my thumb over her shirt found a nipple rising to erection at the touch. With a squeeze and pinch, I took hold of the small bead and rolled it.

Olivia's moan and arching back almost undid me, and quite prepared to have her right there and then, I would have if it wasn't for the dog that bounded over us.

I sat up with a scream as a slobbery tongue covered my face. The owner, a severe-looking man, looked far too pleased with his animal's actions. "Get a room," I heard him mumble after he whistled for his dog, *Fido*, to come.

I sneered at his back and wiped slobber off my face. Looking down to see if Olivia was as indignant as I, I found her smiling at me. This smile I didn't know. I've seen the doctor smile. The caring smile. The sarcastic smile, but this one…I shuddered and my stomach flopped. I'd do anything to see that on her face, and judging by her next expression, she knew it, too. That smile was a deadly weapon.

Chapter Twelve

Spring break came and went and knee-deep in May, I found myself alone in the apartment studying one Sunday night. Olivia had become obsessed with attending seminars, and while I went along to a few, I couldn't get excited by genetic-level virus attacks. Olivia, who had become warier since that picnic date, hadn't given me that deadly smile again. In fact, she hadn't smiled at all. At the increased rate we were studying, I hoped it was more a case of the unavailability of time and not a lack of willingness.

Yawning and stretching, I considered my options for the remainder of the evening. I wasn't working at Sunny's that night, which usually meant a rapid-fire study session to catch up and consolidate notes. After doing exactly that for four hours straight, I was over it. It was only nine, and I wasn't expecting Olivia until after ten. Already in my pajamas, I curled up on the couch and stared mindlessly at the TV for an hour. Ten soon became eleven, and then at the stroke of midnight, my worry kicked in.

Grabbing my cell, I text Olivia.

Hey Liv. You fall asleep at the seminar or something?

I waited and got no reply. Calling her Liv should have irked her into response. Frowning, I dialed her number.

"Babe!" she answered loudly. There was music and voices in the background.

I looked at my phone to make sure I dialed the right person because it was going to be a cold day in hell when Olivia was going to call me babe. I arched my eyebrows to see I had the right number. "Olivia?"

"Come drink with me!" she shouted.

"Uh…what?" I frowned and looked over at the massive calendar on the wall. We had an eight-thirty lecture in the morning before an afternoon of lab work. More poignantly, Olivia didn't drink. *Ever.*

"Come on," she whined. Olivia never whined either.

"Where are you?"

"The Squealing Pig."

I blinked. She was at a bar? A loud, noisy one.

"Kara is here. Say hi, Kara."

A new voice came on the line. "Hey, Darce. Your girlfriend is a riot."

I pinched myself. I *had* to be dreaming this. "Ow."

"Huh?" Olivia said.

"Liv, why are you at a bar with Kara past midnight?"

Olivia groaned. "God, are you doing the mother routine?"

"No, I'm doing the 'who are you and what have you done with my girlfriend' routine."

Olivia made a grunting sound. "Whatever. Come or not. I don't care. I have Kara."

The dial tone sounded in my ear, and I think I was dressed and jogging towards my girlfriend in record time. Thankfully she had chosen to get herself wrecked in a bar only minutes from our front door.

I burst in and stopped still. There, at the bar was Olivia and Kara giggling at one another. Kara's hand sat dangerously on Olivia's thigh. *What the heck was going on?*

I charged over and knocked Kara's hand away.

"Sweetheart," Olivia said, launching into my arms and kissing me soundly.

"Umm…" I said when she stopped kissing me with her whiskey-tasting mouth. I couldn't help it, but that taste burned all the way down to my panties. Clearing my throat and ignoring how easily I was turned on, I glanced at Kara.

"Hi, sexy," she said with a wink.

I quickly looked back at Olivia, expecting some kind of jealous retribution. Instead, she said, "She is, isn't she." Olivia looked me over. "She has no idea what she does to me." She moved the hand she already had on my waist and cupped my backside with a squeeze. I yelped. Kara did the same on the other cheek and I backed away from the pair of them.

"You don't drink," I said to Olivia.

"I do. Just not very often."

"So why tonight?"

Olivia's drunken carefree grin slipped and revealed the pain behind her mask. A surge of protectiveness overwhelmed me, and I ignored her empty remark about how she felt like letting her hair down for once. The Olivia I know is so in control she practically has her bodily functions scheduled to within a five-minute margin. This Olivia looked...*wrong*.

"Come on, we're going home." I took her by the waist and helped her slip from the bar stool.

"What? No. Kara and I—"

"Have had enough." Olivia protested physically, and I fought to retain my grip on her waist.

I changed tactics. "Liv, take me home," I said, adding a wink and licking my lips.

The grin that blossomed on her face made me swallow.

"Can I come too?" Kara asked.

Olivia and I turned to her and said in unison, "No."

Kara pouted.

Olivia patted her arm and dropped a kiss on her cheek. Olivia may not have been feeling jealous, but I sure the hell was, and tugged my girlfriend away from the woman. "Bye, Kara."

My playful, flirtatious, drunken girlfriend swapped personalities when we entered our apartment. Expecting I was going to have to fend her off, instead, she burst into tears and scared the life out of me.

"Shit. Liv? Are you okay?" I wrapped my arms around her only to be pushed back against the wall.

"Don't! Please. Just don't touch me."

"Ah...okay?"

She glared at me for a moment, before sighing and staring at her boot-clad feet. "Sorry. But I need to be alone tonight."

And with those words, she stalked off and shut our bedroom door leaving me in no doubt I was spending a night on the couch. I glanced at my old room. Or perhaps the single bed. It turns out it didn't matter where I slept. I could hear Olivia crying, and desperate to see her, I hovered by her door, hand on the doorknob, willing her to call for me. She never did, and when her sobbing tapered off, I rested against the door, eyes closed and wishing I knew the answers to this new puzzle. It was obvious she was hurting, but why was a different conundrum.

Chancing my luck, I cracked open her door to find her with a small bottle of whiskey in her hand and passed out on her bed that was littered with photographs. The lamp on her side table glowed peacefully over her tight-balled form. She was still dressed in a jacket, jeans and boots, and deciding to make her more comfortable, I went to her.

Scooping up some of the photos, I gasped when I saw them. In the pictures, was a young Olivia cradling a baby dressed in blue. A smile glowed on her face and a young man hovered over her shoulders in some shots looking equally as pleased. I pressed a hand over my chest. *Olivia had a child?* I gasped, staring at her peaceful face. She blinked her eyes open and smiled drunkenly at me. "You have a son?" I asked, still shocked by that piece of information.

She noticed what I was holding and peace flew right out the window. "Get out!" she screamed. Clumsily snatching the photograph from my hand, she scooped the rest into a messy pile. "Get out of my room."

Something in me cracked under the rejection. She was hurting and all I wanted to do was comfort her, however, I suspected if I went near her she might bite or something worse. Still, I wasn't leaving. "Where is he? Where is your son?"

Olivia's face crumpled and my heart broke as I read the truth in that expression. "You have no right to ask me that."

"I have every right."

"No, you don't." Olivia stood and had screamed those words in my face. I stepped back at the vehemence of it.

"Wrong. I'm your girlfriend. We're supposed to lo—*like* each other, trust each other, and support each other when we need it most. Why won't you let me help you?"

"Because I don't need it, and I don't need you!"

I gasped and stepped backward.

Olivia's chin wobbled. "I don't need anybody."

I shook my head. "You're lying."

"I've been alone my whole life, Darcy. I know exactly what I do and don't need, and what I don't want is someone to pity me. You were a bad idea from the start."

My heart thumped and ached. "You're not the ideal choice either, but I love you anyway." The fact I just declared my love to her barely registered in her eyes, but my heart began to beat crazy fast as I recognized the truth in my words.

Olivia's following laugh sounded cruel and hollow. "I'm no one's ideal choice. Don't forget I know I'm not who you really want."

"What?"

She waved me off. "Don't worry, Darce, that colorless little Taylor will be on the market soon enough."

"Taylor?" I shook my head. "I don't want Taylor, I want *you.*"

"Only because she found someone else."

"No. Because I found *you.* Can't you see that?" I huffed and ran a hand through my hair. "I have *no* idea what I'm doing. I don't know how to make you see you can trust me. I'm on your side."

"For how long? Huh? Until you find someone else? Someone easier?"

I think I may have growled. Stubborn didn't come close to describing this woman. "I don't want anyone else." I moved over to her and took her shoulder in my hands. "You're a complicated, difficult woman, but I'm still here."

"You shouldn't be."

I sighed through my nose. "I know."

"I can't do this anymore." She stepped away from me. "I don't want this complication."

I blinked. "Complication? That's what you see me as? Some kind of problem?"

She didn't answer and evaded my eyes.

My lip trembled. "You don't want me." It was a statement and she didn't respond. My throat closed up, but somehow I managed to say, "Okay. Have it your way. If you really don't need me, I'll stay out of your way."

She swallowed.

"Liv?" I was desperate for some kind of answer. Negative or positive. The silence was uncomfortable.

"My name is *Olivia*."

My lungs burned. "Of course it is." I turned and left, leaving her standing frozen beside her bed and those cataclysmic photographs. I didn't want to leave. I wanted to wrap her close to me. To tell her everything was going to be all right, but I didn't know how.

Walking into my old room, I closed the door and slid down the back of it to the floor. I was in too much shock to cry, but my face burned with pain. Staring blankly at the pillow-less bed in front of me, my phone vibrated in my pocket.

It was a text from Taylor. Why was she texting me at one in the morning? *Did you see the game? Just got back from the after party. So gr8!*

I responded. *No. Just broke up with Liv.*

My phone rang a second later. "What happened?" Taylor asked.

I shrugged. "I don't know."

"She dumped you, didn't she? Bitch."

I shook my head. "I think I dumped her."

"What?"

I let out a long shaky breath. *How do I undo what I just did?*

"Is it…" Taylor started.

"Hmm?"

"Is it because of me?"

I frowned. *Because of her?* "Huh?"

"Did you break up with her because you had, you know…feelings for me?"

My head dropped back against the door and as I shut my eyes, I shook my head. "No, Taylor. I don't have feelings for you anymore."

"Oh." Silence. "Then why did you break up?"

"I wish I knew." And really, there was only one way I was going to find out. "Look, I gotta go."

"Darce?"

"Talk to you later." I hung up on Taylor and stood. A little woozy, I opened my door and walked back to Olivia's room. She was still standing, staring at the photos on the bed. Her puffy-eyed stare turned to me as I crossed the room. "Hey," I whispered.

Her lip trembled, breaking my heart all over again. She looked isolated, frantic, and ready to implode on herself. I wasn't having any of that, so I held out my arms and she fell into them with an ease that surprised us both. Heavy choking sobs erupted from her thin frame, and we both collapsed to the floor under their weight. Clueless, scared, but determined, I held the fragile woman until she passed out in my lap. Pulling a pillow and blanket from the bed, I gently nudged her head onto the feather-filled cushioning and covered her body. The photos fell to the floor with my efforts, and I picked them up.

Unable to help my curiosity, I looked at the remaining pictures as she slumbered. The sequence was aged-based as the baby began to grow and crawl, and slowly, the man slipped from the photographs. The baby, still in diapers, was suddenly covered in tubes and tape and had an incision over his chest that I recognized as the result of some serious pediatric surgery. I covered my mouth as I found a death certificate confirming the worst. Jayden David Boyd was ten months old when he passed away. Harder still was to find he shared the same birthday as me.

"Oh, God," I whispered, and feeling terribly guilty I'd just uncovered a secret Olivia had never disclosed. Wiping tears from my eyes, I stacked them together and placed them on the side table. I laid down beside her and cried quietly for the pain she must have endured. Her reasons for going into pediatrics because no child should feel pain made a significant amount of sense. I tucked myself alongside her and wrapped my arm around her. She snuggled against me, and for the rest of the night, I held the woman close.

એઝ

I woke on the floor a few hours later with Olivia still in my arms and staring at me in confusion in the early morning light.

"Why are we sleeping on the floor like dogs?"

Her voice was hoarse and her eyes bloodshot, so her snide tone didn't come across. I brushed a strand of hair behind her ear. "How are you?"

She swallowed and looked away. "I've been better." After a sigh, she said, "I need to shower."

I nodded at her, smelling the sweat, alcohol, and smoke on her from last night. That combination must have made her innate sense of cleanliness crazy. She gave me a pointed glare and I squeaked. "Oh. Sorry." Letting her go from my koala grip, she stood and then noticed the photos on the side table. It was obvious I moved them. She bit her lip and looked at me.

I stood. "Coffee?" She wasn't fooled.

"What did you see?" she asked. I could see the blood-red veins in the whites of her eyes. The dark smudge of skin below them. The sadness deep inside those eyes. I doubted she wanted me to know the reasons behind that look.

I glanced at the side table and looked back at her as she appraised me. Her eyes crinkled and narrowed as she watched me. I reached out and took her hand. With a gentle squeeze, I said, "Nothing I'm going to ask about until you're ready. It's not my business."

She lifted her chin. "That's right, it isn't."

That stung, but really, it wasn't up to me to pressure her into telling me her sorrowful history, as much as I wished I could. What I could do, is make sure she understood I was in her corner. I raised my hand to her cheek and stroked the skin there. "You're an amazing woman, and you intimidate the hell out of me, but I love you and I'm staying right here."

Olivia blinked and took a shuddery breath. My declaration looked like it impacted this time. "Thank you," she whispered.

"Go shower."

She nodded vacantly and shut herself into the bathroom.

I yawned and rubbed at my scratchy eyes. It was going to be a long day.

Chapter Thirteen

Whatever progress we had made as a couple took a step back as Olivia began to avoid me over the following weeks. It was like I'd lifted the curtain to a hurt she tried to avoid and defensively pushed me away to save herself. My own mood shifted from buoyant to depressed as I accommodated her need for isolation. I took more shifts at the dry cleaner, I studied at the library, and I moved out of her bed to take up residence in my neglected single one. Studying at home was eerie and silent as I did my utmost to be quiet and diligent. Before we realized it, the weather was warm and we'd completed the first twelve months of med school and had nothing left to do but wait for our results, take summer vacation, and quietly panic about the upcoming years.

Summer vacation at Harvard Medical with the new Pathway program in place meant just over two weeks of relaxation before three intensive years of medical training commenced. With the coming years of clinical study, I planned to utilize my two weeks off wisely. I was going to tinker with my car, catch up with Taylor and her girlfriend, and most likely pine for Olivia.

The woman, whose company I missed, had yet to inform me of her vacation plans. Knowing her, she was going to do work experience under one of the lecturers.

As for me, I was leaving tomorrow afternoon for Minnesota to enjoy the last day of July with my parents.

I sighed heavy and long.

"What is it?" Olivia asked, breaking the silence and making me jolt.

"Huh?" I looked over my shoulder from the couch to see her frowning at me. She didn't look annoyed for once. I guess with study officially over, she wasn't so uptight.

"What's wrong?"

I shook my head. "Nothing. I'm just thinking of vacation."

"Oh."

"Do you know what you're doing yet?"

She shook her head at me. "You?"

"Just hanging out at home, I guess."

"You'll be seeing Taylor?"

I nodded.

"Are we taking a break then?"

"*What?* Why?" My heart rate skyrocketed.

Olivia looked back to her desk where she had spread next year's study schedule and shrugged. I frowned at her, my mind processing. I told her almost a month ago I was going home for the school break, and now that I thought about it, she'd become quieter since then. I had broken that news in the week following her drinking session. She had been reclusive as she was obviously mourning a son who should have been turning seven soon. Psychology wasn't my forte, but I got a sudden clarity of mind. *Did she think I was running away from her?*

"Olivia?"

"Mmm?"

"Look at me."

She did turn eventually and glanced at me from the corner of her eye.

I clicked my tongue at her and got up from the couch, spun her chair and planted my hands on the arm rest of her office chair. "I don't want a break from you."

She took a long inhale through her nose. "Okay."

"And I definitely don't want Taylor. I thought I'd already clarified that."

"Okay."

"I want *you.*" She closed her eyes and let her head tilt forward as she sucked in a harsh breath. I tipped her chin back up with a finger. "Olivia. I want you."

She looked back at me and I barely caught her whispered word: "Why?"

I gasped. She looked so vulnerable. Her blue eyes shined with unshed tears and she looked hopelessly lost. My hand trailed from her chin to her cheek and I brushed her skin with my thumb. "Because you're beautiful, smart, determined, anal, bitchy, ambitious and caring." Olivia had stiffened at some of my words of choice, but she remained silent. "Because you challenge me. Because you try to make me better. You taught me to cook, you make me accountable, and you're amazing. You're exasperating. I want you because I love you. I wish I could prove to you that you can trust me. That I'm here and never leaving by choice. That you're everything I want. I know I'm terrible at relationships, but I'm willing to learn." I took a deep breath. *Here I go.* Leaning closer to her, I whispered, "Let me in."

Olivia's jaw clenched as she bit down on her back teeth. "I don't know how."

"Then step-by-step we try…together. I'm not giving up on this."

Olivia's eyes were wide and vulnerable as she stared at me and the subtle shift in power was surprising. I was the strong one. I was the sure, confident one. I was the key to unlocking this. It was time for me to woman-up.

Swallowing, I reached out and caressed her cheek. "Please, will you try?" I whispered.

She nodded on a rushed outgoing breath and reached up to kiss me.

We hadn't done this for over a month, and it felt like coming home. She was temptation and passion and I wanted more. The kiss deepened but soon my stance became uncomfortable and I was forced to pull away before I fell over. Pulling her to her feet and we stood there trying to catch our breath. I looked into her hooded eyes and knew it was time. I didn't care if I didn't know what I was doing, I needed to touch her. *All* of her.

Pulling her to me with a hand hooked behind her neck, I moaned into a kiss that was anything but gentle. Tongues warred and hands explored and soon I'd been backed up against the nearest wall. How I ended up like this on most occasions bemused me, but when her leg slipped between mine as Olivia's urgency increased, I found I didn't care.

Tugging at her shirt and hoping she would let me pull it over her head, she stilled my hands and moved back a fraction. My heart dropped to my ankles. Chance gone.

"You're sure?" she whispered to me as she panted.

She hadn't pushed me away. She was still against me. She was looking at me with those lust-filled eyes and wanted more. I swallowed away the sudden dryness in my mouth and nodded frantically. "I'm sure, only—" I stopped and bit my lip. *Only I had no idea what I'm doing.*

She smiled at me. A soft, barely-there, smile that reignited my heart. She leaned in and gave me a gentle kiss. Taking my hand, she drew me into her room, leaving the lights off and letting the illumination in the kitchen filter through the door.

She stopped us beside the bed and lifted her shirt from her body. My mouth went dry and moisture pooled elsewhere as I looked at her semi-naked torso. Nothing but a blood red bra covered her torso, and I just had to touch. Reaching out, I let my knuckles skim across her abdomen and the faint lines I saw there. Evidence of her motherhood. Fascinated by the way her breath hitched and her muscles spasmed, I trailed the hand up, I caressed the skin below her breasts and she filled her lungs, allowing her chest to rise.

I shook my head in reverence. "So beautiful."

She smiled and shook her head at me. The next thing I knew, my top was gone and she was afforded a view of my torso covered with a sports bra. "*This* is beautiful," she said before pulling me close and kissing me urgently. Feeling her skin against mine was incredible. Her body heat warmed me and sent chills down my spine. The contrast was extraordinary. As goosebumps prickled my skin, she ran her hands around the waistband of my favorite pair of jeans, and her knuckles pressed into my abdomen as she unbuttoned them. A tingle ran down my spine, through my apex and right into my toes.

"You're trembling," Olivia whispered against my neck as she unzipped my jeans.

I nodded and tilted my head as she pressed kisses against my skin. Feeling the need to explain myself, I said, "I've never—"

"I know." She kissed me again. A deep, possessive act that left me breathless. I gripped onto her for dear life as she wrapped me tight against her and stole the air from my lungs. My head spun and I was sure I was going to pass out, but then she pulled away, gasping for air like I was. "Please," she said on a rough exhale. "Please tell me you're ready. I can't…" She shook her head.

I cupped her face in my hands, grounding myself. "Make love to me."

Her chest imploded on itself as she let out a rush of relieved air. She nodded at me in the dim light. "That I can do."

Devastating me with another kiss, she gently pushed me to her bed. Our hips seemed to grind and reach for one another without conscious thought, and we danced on the covers in a rhythm of heavy pants and delirious moans. Having her fill of my lips and tongue, Olivia broke away and moved her kisses down my neck and across my collarbones. I shivered at the sensations she was shuttling through my skin. That secret place between my legs was alive and electric, and throbbing mercilessly.

So lost in her touch, I barely registered the way my jeans were moving off my body. It was the lack of warmth against my skin that made me open my eyes. I almost wish I didn't, because I nearly stopped breathing at the sight of Olivia kneeling between my legs. She had stripped off her pants to benefit my eyes with a body that made me gasp. Briefly captured by her hips and the triangle of underwear protecting the region between, I looked up at her and stilled. She was ravishing me with her eyes.

Exposed to her in nothing but my underwear, I held my breath to hear her review. She licked her lips and swallowed. A husky voice followed. "Gorgeous." Hands dropped to my thighs and gently skimmed their way up my body. Olivia was shaking her head. "You have no idea what you do to me. How much it took to deny myself."

I swallowed and her words sunk in. "Deny this?"

She was covering me then. All warmth and soft curves as she smiled down at me. "I've wanted you this way for so long." She leaned down and smattered kisses along my jaw. "I've wanted this…" She shook her head against my neck. Leaning up, she looked at me, almost making sure it was okay for her to confess her secrets. "I've wanted you Darcy, and now…I can have you."

I smiled at her and brushed my fingers over her cheek. It bemused me to realize Olivia knew I wasn't ready for this before now. I may have been aching to have my first orgasm, but it would have only sated my body, not my heart. I had been stuck in a naïve cycle of infatuation, desperation, and confusion, but now I was a woman in love. Now I was a woman fighting for the only thing I needed…Olivia. Today, I had asked her to be mine, and in turn, I wanted to be hers. "Then take me," I whispered, sounding far more confident than I felt. I may have taken charge of my destiny, but I was still very nervous.

She smiled. A genuine, loving, glorious smile that made me catch my breath. And then she nodded. "Okay."

Her hands, warm and slender, felt like they were everywhere at once. My breasts arched under her touch as she teased my nipples to intense arousal. Reaching below me to the bed, she caught the band of my sports bra and yanked it upwards, almost dislocating my shoulders in the process. About to query her urgency, I got my answer when she descended upon my breasts with lips and tongue and a moan that wet my remaining underwear. Bare-chested and shameless, I ran my fingers through her hair as I pressed against her mouth with an arch of my back.

I was lost in perfumes of vanilla and jasmine, and the moist warmth of her tongue. Uncaring, I heard myself mutter her name and brief words of encouragement. A chuckle shook her before she lowered her mouth to the other breast.

Her touch shivered through my skin as it brushed over my ribs, down the curve of my waist and over my hips. I rose against her touch and involuntarily jerked against her fingers as they explored below my panty line. A kissed dropped against the expanse between belly button and underwear made me moan and seconds later, I was stripped of my last piece of armor.

I was shaking when she covered me again. Her leg between mine and her breath warm against my face. "You okay?" she whispered.

I was more than okay. I was feverish for her. I swallowed and nodded, certain that my voice was long ago rendered useless with passion. She smiled again and stroked my cheek. Her mouth against mine once more, she darted her tongue between my lips as she tried to distract me from the way her fingers danced over my hip. Sweeping her tongue across my teeth, I broke away and cried out as she touched my intimate parts for the first time.

"Oh, my...Liv," I said in hoarse pants of air.

Moaning on each touch, she began to circle the most sensitive part of me with a long finger. She rolled her hips against me and tucked her head into my neck. The moment she bit down on my pulse point, I lifted off the bed and provoked the most sensational moan from her when my thigh pressed hard against a hot slickness I recognized as her sex. *Oh, God. I did that to her. I made her that aroused.* My next goal was to make her moan like that again.

I had been clutching at her arm and back without logic when she began to stroke between my legs. Now, still pressing against her delicious touch, I made a deliberate attempt to touch her with purpose. One hand draping down her back squeezed at her buttocks and pulled her tight against my leg as I lifted it.

Her appreciation was instant and she whispered my name against my skin and rolled her pelvis down against me.

I congratulated myself for my success.

Sucking in air as she rubbed harder against me with her fingers, I did my best to retain my concentration as my other hand skimmed up her side, found its way between our bodies, and squeezed her breast.

"Darcy," she murmured. A murmur that became a sensual groan as I pinched the hard little tip of her breast between forefinger and thumb.

I forgot everything I was doing when her hand dropped lower and pressed at my entrance. I'd never been touched by anyone, and everything she was doing was beyond anything I could dream. I froze as she explored me with shallow, gentle probes. My hips canted and I moaned as a long finger sheathed itself inside me.

I hissed with the sharp sting of penetration before that gave away to pleasure. "Oh, Lord. Liv, that's…oh…" I trailed off with another moan of appreciation.

Her finger began to slide in and out of me and so overwhelmed with the sensation, that I forgot everything. My breath faltered, my heart stopped, and I could do nothing but search for more of her touch with an arch of my hips.

"Oh, Liv…" She hummed against my neck and eased another long finger inside me, curling her fingers upwards and doing something to me that lifted my hips from the bed. "God!"

She raised her head from my neck and looked down at me. I tried to keep my eyes open, but the more she thrust and the more I rose against her hand, the more fanatical I became. Coiling at the base of my spine was this awareness I'd never felt before. I grasped at her buttocks and pulled her close as she leaned above me, using her weight to encourage her fingers deeper. My other hand, long having lost its grip on her breast, reached for her as well and as she pressed down on my hips, I thrust up against hers. With a keening cry, I felt that coil build into a pressure I wasn't sure I could withstand, and as she drove me insane with her ministrations, my consciousness burst and I cried out as my body exploded to pieces. Thrashing against Olivia, I tried to make sense of what happened, and before I could, my mind went blank and sated.

I came to with a shiver and felt Olivia caressing the skin at my side with long, languid strokes.

"Hi," she whispered.

"Hi."

Smiling, she kissed my shoulder. "You okay?"

I nodded. I was more than okay. I was sky high on endorphins. "You?"

She hummed against my skin. Her thigh rubbed against mine and she fidgeted her hips. I blinked rapidly as I realized what that might mean. I shuffled to my side, dislodging her a little. My hand rested on her hip and drew itself up her body to her neck, which I used to draw her in for a kiss. "You're amazing."

She chuckled and shook her head. "No. You're the amazing one. You're magnificent."

I blushed.

She smiled.

"I want to…" I cleared my throat. "I want to touch you."

She shuddered a little. "You don't have to."

"Oh." I nibbled on my lip. I really really wanted to touch her. To make her feel the way she made me feel. To show her how much I cared for her. Her fingers stroking my cheek roused me from my thoughts. Those blue eyes of hers looked desperate, and I couldn't decide what it was she wanted, so I said, "I *need* to touch you." She drew in a breath. "Please?"

After she exhaled, she nodded. "I really wish you would."

That was enough for me, and I closed the gap to kiss her. Taking control of the encounter, I plundered her mouth with my tongue as I rolled on top of her. The moan she emanated was delicious and trickled down my skin straight to the juncture between my legs. I couldn't believe I was turned on already. Choosing not to question the way this woman made me feel, I let my fantasies come to life. I had long dreamt of the way I would touch a lover. Of the way I would make them squirm. Of the way they would taste on my tongue. For months, I had imagined doing this to Olivia.

Descending down her body with nibbling teeth and soothing tongue, I pulled her panties away and inhaled the arousal I had induced. It was musky and sweet and with a swipe of my tongue, I coated my senses in its taste.

Olivia hissed and arched her back, pressing the hard bundle of nerves against my tongue. Wrapping my lips around it, I sucked and tore a long moan from her lips. Looking up her body, I saw the bend in her back and the way her breasts strained against her bra. I saw the tendons pulled tight in her neck as her teeth bared in pleasure.

My senses fired in bursts of electricity, and suddenly I was fumbling. I'd never had this much power and I was overwhelmed at how submissive Olivia was at my touch. She was at my mercy and I didn't want to disappoint. Unfortunately, now that I was conscious of being perfect, I became clumsy and nervous.

I continued to lick and wanted to provide her with more sensation and misjudged how much my hands were shaking. She hissed as I accidentally scraped her skin as my finger tried to part those velvet curtains at her entrance. Her head lifted and her hand touched my hair.

"S-sorry," I stuttered. "I...uh...damn it."

She smiled at me and ran her fingers through my hair. "Come here."

I nodded and did what I was told. "Relax," she said after kissing her taste from my lips. "Relax."

I nodded against her forehead and took a deep breath. Kissing her again, I let my hand cup her and stroke the moisture from her center. Rolling over the tight engorged bud above her entrance, I circled it in smooth taunting movements, and once again, she was putty at my touch.

"I'm so close," she murmured into my mouth. "Please, Darcy. I need more."

I acknowledged her words with a moan and tried once again to penetrate her with my finger. Successful, I slid it deep within her, careful not to snag her sensitive skin with my nails again. She rolled against me and with her keening whimper, I pushed in another finger. Her breath rushed from her body with significant force and she bit down hard on her lip. Groaning, she sucked air in with short, sharp breaths and the tempo increased exponentially as I felt her walls begin to clench. I was lost in the feeling of her. The way her muscles drew my fingers in deeper. The way her body heated below mine. The way our skin rubbed together and the way she began to pant my name as her body tensed.

In a moment of complete stillness after I curled my fingers like she had, she grunted a high-pitch sound and shuddered in my arms. Clutching me upon her, I let my weight drop and allowed her body to continue pulsing and rubbing against mine.

"Oh, Darcy," she whispered as her heart rate calmed many minutes later. "You are simply divine."

"I did okay?" I asked, unsure as I lifted my head to look at her.

She chuckled. "You did more than okay, trust me."

I grinned. Happy with my first attempt at making love, Olivia shook her head at me and encouraged me to climb under the bed sheets with her. Cozy and satiated, we wrapped our naked bodies together and drifted into a deep slumber. Dreams of Olivia's smile and moaning gasps filled my sleep. I was sure I slept with a smile on my face.

Chapter Fourteen

I now see the logic behind declining your sexual urges as Olivia had. However, how she had managed to deny herself considering she had an inclination of what it might be like when we made love was mind-boggling. I was blissfully unaware of the amount of self-control she had. Until now. Now, I was frustrated, always on edge, and damn near ready to explode if I couldn't have her naked in my arms within the next hour. I had gone from twenty-three-year-old virgin to raging nymphomaniac.

It took little-to-no convincing to have Olivia join me for the two-week summer break. It was dawning on me that she had no one in her life to visit and lived a secluded life. Assimilating her into my family was easy, and somewhere inside me, I recognized I was giving her a taste of what it was like to have people that loved you unconditionally.

My parents certainly did that.

Ecstatic that Olivia was coming to stay, I had been abruptly shoved to the side as favorite daughter, and Olivia had been tucked firmly under my mother's wing from the instant we arrived. A problematic position considering I had a constant urge to rip Olivia's clothes off.

We had crashed dreamlessly together late last night, exhausted from the travel and beginning stanzas of our love-making marathon in Boston. I had woken to her familiar scent for the first time in weeks and felt my body instantly respond. Moving my hands over her body, I was progressively initiating more and more moans from her when my door knocked and mom burst in a millisecond after.

"Oh!" she said, noticing the guilty looks on our faces. Mom blushed while I hid under the covers and pretended I didn't just have my hand in Olivia's panties. "I guess I should rethink that," Mom said. I assumed she indicated to the door and her entrance style, but I couldn't tell, I was still hiding.

Olivia began to shake with silent laughter as I heard my door shut.

Knock. Knock. Knock. "You decent?" Mom called out.

"Yes, Mrs. Wright. Please come in," Olivia called back.

"Now, dear, Mrs. Wright was my mother-in-law and I detested that demon with each breath I took. Call me Marg or Ma."

I poked my head out of the covers. Did my mother just instruct my girlfriend to call her Mom? I looked at Olivia. She looked shocked. "Ah…okay…Marg," she said.

Mom grinned. "Now, Darcy dear, I'm going to Duluth today and I'm going to steal your girlfriend away."

"What? Why?"

"Because it's none of your business, that's why."

"But, Mom," I said, hearing the girly whine in my voice. Olivia smirked at me.

"It's not negotiable. Olivia, dear, we're leaving in half an hour."

"Yes, ma'am," she said, smiling at my mother. After smiling back, she shut the door and we could hear her whistling her way downstairs.

"What's in Duluth?"

"Boats."

Olivia screwed her face up at me, and before I knew it, she had left with Mom leaving me frustrated and alone. Dad had gone to work as the sun rose, and after moping about in the kitchen, I spotted a box in the corner boasting auto parts.

I smiled.

Mavis.

Dashing upstairs to put on my overalls, I busied myself in the garage reacquainting myself with my car.

∞

Elbow deep in grease and growling at a split bolt deep inside the engine, I stood and threw the spanner in the general direction of the tool box.

"Ah!"

Spinning, I realized I just missed Taylor as she walked through the shed door. "Sorry. You okay?"

She held a hand to her chest and nodded at me. "What the hell are you doing?"

"Mavis is being a bitch today."

Taylor smiled and shook her head. "When isn't she?"

I bit my lip. "True."

Taylor's smile grew and she moved closer to me, leaning in and kissing my cheek. "You didn't tell me you were here already," she said as she leaned back. "In fact, I haven't heard from you since Thursday. You okay?"

She was right. I was messaging her the night I confronted Olivia about her mood. Taylor was aware of the troubles we'd been having since the night Olivia drank herself to sleep. *Aware* was probably a strong word. She knew I was back in my old room and moping about. In the past thirty-six hours, however, I was completely obsessed with naked Olivia and had yet to share that news with my best friend. I sighed and smiled thinking of the way Olivia looked laying back on the bed ready for me.

"Uh. Darce?"

"Hmm?"

"Where did you just go?"

"Huh?" I cleared my throat. "Nowhere."

Taylor narrowed her eyes. "So, how's the girlfriend?"

"Olivia?"

"How many girlfriends do you have?"

I smiled. "Just one, and she's great."

Taylor arched her eyebrows. "I thought you two were having…issues."

I shook my head. "We sorted it out." I grinned. "And she came home for vacation."

Taylor's mouth dropped open. "She's *here?*"

"Duluth, actually. Mom kidnaped her." I smiled as I thought of the interaction in my bedroom that morning. "Mom asked her to call her Ma."

"She what? I mean...that's great, right?"

"Yeah, it is." Taking a deep breath, I said, "Where's Charli?"

"At work."

"And you're both good?"

Taylor shrugged. "I guess."

I nodded and we fell into an awkward sort of silence. I wasn't used to this. Taylor was the one person I could rely on to feel comfortable, but this was far from it.

"So..." Taylor started.

"So..."

"I...uh...probably should get back. I just wanted to drop by and say hi."

"Oh, okay."

Taylor nodded her head. "See you at dinner? Your parents invited us over yesterday, you know, for the special occasion."

"Cool. See you then."

We smiled at each other and she left. I watched her leave with a chilling trepidation growing in my chest. *What just happened?*

Worse still, Taylor had just reminded me that today was my birthday. The reason my mother had dragged Olivia into Duluth suddenly dawned on me. There's only one thing my mother goes to Duluth for...cheesecake.

℘

Mavis continued to mock me, but I ignored her. Gone was my frustration with the bolt, replaced by the fear that Olivia was vulnerable to another breakdown. I saw how she dealt with the anniversary of Jayden's death, so how was she going to cope with the anniversary of the day he was born. I should have warned her.

"Ugh. Idiot."

"Pardon?"

"Shit!" I jumped and banged my head on the hard edge as I tried to stand. "Ow! Ow! Ow!" I rubbed my head.

"Jesus, Darcy, stand still." It was Olivia. Grabbing my shoulders, she stilled me and tipped my head into the light hanging from the raised hood. "You'll live. You've just nicked the scalp." She turned my head to her with a hand under my chin. "I suggest you stop rubbing oil into it, though."

I winced under the throbbing in my head and studied her. She looked calm. Tentatively, I asked, "How was Duluth?"

She shrugged. "It was fine. How was…" she looked at my car.

"Mavis."

"How was Mavis?"

"She was a bitch. There's a split bolt down there," I pointed to the bottom of the engine. "And I think there's a blockage in the fuel line. I was just trying to see the best way to manage that without having to pull it all out."

"Mmm."

I smiled at the way she bulged her eyes in some kind of mocking gesture. If she was being snide, maybe she was okay? "I guess car talk doesn't turn you on?"

She shook her head. "Sorry. No."

"What *does* turn you on?" I smiled and stepped closer to her.

She stepped back. "Girlfriends that aren't covered in black soot and oil."

I quickly pushed my overalls down to my boots, revealing a sports bra and boy shorts.

She looked over my body with an appreciative gaze. Swallowing, she said, "Your hands are still greasy."

"I don't need to use my hands, remember?" I enjoyed the flush moving up Olivia's neck and felt a rush to make her feel good.

"Your parents are just over there." She indicated to the house ninety feet away.

"I have a car."

"What? No." Leaning in, I nuzzled her neck with my nose. She huffed and raised her chin up as I began pressing kisses along her flesh. I was comforted to see she was as affected as I was when we touched. And really, when I thought about it, she always had, however, she had once regained enough control to walk away. Now, I hoped that control had gone.

"Sit in the car," I said against her throat. Feeling her swallow beneath my lips, she started to shake her head. "Now," I said, sucking hard against her pulse point.

The driver's seat was easily accessible considering the doors were leaning against the garage walls. She sat on the dusty leather and looked up at me with darkened eyes. I looked at her skirt and said, "Off."

She glowered at me for a moment, before hiking her skirt to her hips.

"Unless you want greasy panties, take them off."

She was scowling when she did as I requested. "I find this highly unsanitary."

And I didn't care. Dropping to my knees, I pressed my face against the flushed skin she revealed and made her forget all about sanitary environments. As promised, I didn't touch her with my greasy hands, and because of her expert instruction on our first night of making love, I guided her writhing form to the crevasse and pushed her promptly off. It was quick, it was satisfying, and I was exuding arrogance as I smiled up at her when she recovered from her climax.

Balanced precariously on the edge of my own orgasm, I could see she was willing to repay the favor, and the way she tugged me to her for a kiss, I was flooding with anticipation.

"Darcy?"

I yelped. That was my dad. I heard the screen door of the house close. "Crap." Scrambling off Olivia, I tripped over my sagging overalls as I tried to pull them up and landed flat on my back.

"Darce?" Dad said, walking into the shed and frowning at me.

"Just taking a time out," I said, noticing a colony of cobwebs on the ceiling.

"Olivia?"

I looked over to see Dad had spotted my girlfriend sitting in the driver's seat. She had managed to yank her skirt down, and she stood, dusty from the seat, and nodded at him. "David."

Dad looked between the pair of us, confused, and then we all noticed simultaneously that Olivia's red panties were lying on the ground next to me.

"Oh!" Dad said. "Umm…"

I swiped at the panties and tucked them out of sight. Scrambling off the ground, I said, "I checked out the engine."

Dad blinked.

"I think I need to check the fuel line."

Dad went bright pink and glanced at Olivia. He whispered to me, "Ah, Darce, honey, I'm not sure that's information you should be sharing with me."

"What?" My eyes widened and I gasped. "No! Not *Olivia's* engine, that one!" I pointed under the hood. "God, why would you—*why?*" I shook my head wondering how the hell Dad got so off-topic. I hid behind my hands and groaned. "Oh, my God."

Dad cleared his throat. "Yes, well…umm." He turned and practically sprinted from the garage. "A tie on the doorknob next time please!" he yelled at me from the back steps.

I remained shaking my head.

"Need to service the fuel line, huh?" Olivia whispered soft and low in my ear.

I shivered. "Don't you start. I'm mortified!"

"Just imagine, he could have caught you *servicing* me."

I gaped at Olivia and her amused grin as she walked back to the house, leaving me in a state of abject humiliation, and keen arousal. Groaning, I hung my head. "My life isn't fair, Mavis."

∞

Degreased and unable to meet my father's eye, we sat around the kitchen table a little later with Taylor and her parents. Charli was notably absent, and Taylor looked depressed.

"So, dears, how was your first year at medical school," Mrs. Robbins asked us.

"Good. I passed." I shoveled more of my mom's meatloaf in my mouth and smiled.

"You *passed*?" Olivia said. Turning to Mrs. Robbins, she said, "Unbeknownst to a majority of the community, Darcy is exceptionally bright. She finished in the top five of the class. Just." Olivia gave me a rueful glare after that. I had been as shocked as her when I just topped her at the overall results.

I smiled at her.

"That's wonderful dear," Mrs. Robbins said. My mother and father beamed and Taylor gave me a congratulatory wink. "Just think, a couple more years and you'll be back here with your smarts making us all better," Mrs. Robbins said.

I nodded.

"With her grades, Darcy has the potential to make significant headway in the medical profession. Wherever that may be." Olivia sipped at her water as everyone paused.

"You're not coming back here?" Taylor said.

"What?" I put down my fork.

"Your girlfriend just said you're not coming home."

"No, she didn't."

"She may as well have. You're too smart for us now?"

"What? No."

Taylor stood. "Good luck to you." And with that, she walked out of the door.

What the heck?

Jumping up, I chased her without thought. Taylor had nearly reached her car when I called out to her. "Wait."

She turned and said, "What?"

"What's wrong with us?"

Taylor shook her head. "I don't know."

"Have I done something wrong?"

Taylor shook her head. "No, I have."

"What?"

"Charli and I broke up last night."

"What? Why?"

"I told her about what happened at Christmas this afternoon."

I frowned and cocked my head.

"I told her I kissed you."

I gasped.

"She knew you were coming back for summer vacation and said if I wanted you, I could have you and she walked out."

"Oh, Tay." I walked over and wrapped my arms around her. She rested her head on my shoulder and started to cry. "Do you still love her?"

Taylor nodded against my shirt. Her affirmation made me smile. Gone was the pain it once induced. Gone was the heartache. Gone was my infatuation with my friend, and in its place, a sympathy and desire for her to hold the one she loved.

"Then tell her," I whispered into her hair.

She shook her head. "She won't believe me. She thinks I want you."

I pulled my head back. "Do you?"

Taylor's red-rimmed eyes brimmed with salty tears. "I don't know. I'm so confused."

I shook my head at her. "You're not in love with me, Tay."

"But what if I was?"

Sighing heavily, I kissed her cheek. "It's too late."

Taylor stepped out of my embrace. "Because of Olivia." It was spat out like fact.

"Yeah. Because of Olivia."

Taylor took a deep breath. "Your mom never asked me to call her Ma."

I blinked as that information settled in. Taylor had known my parents her entire life. They were essentially her second family, and always would be.

Before I had a chance to reply, Taylor shook her head. "Sorry. I…I don't mean…" She huffed.

"You're jealous?"

"I have every right to be!" Taylor snapped suddenly. "She's stealing you away from us. Away from *me*."

I flinched. "Come on, Tay. You don't mean that."

Taylor paced a little, shaking her head. She ran a hand through her hair. "I'm sorry. It's just…I'm so used to being the only one you needed, you know. All we ever dreamed about was growing old together by the lake, and now…I don't know what the hell you want. I don't know how to deal with this."

"Deal with what."

"You and *her*."

I narrowed my eyes. "Olivia is my partner, Tay."

"Really? Because as far as I recall, you used her to make me jealous."

"That was a long time ago, and you know it. Things have changed."

"Have they? Really?"

I stepped in front of her. "Look, I might have started out pretending to be in a relationship with Olivia, but everything about her and I is real now. I loved you for such a long time, and I would have been yours forever if you'd only shown me you were interested, but now it's too late. You fell for Charli and I accepted I could never have you."

"So you chose leftovers?"

I slapped Taylor. A strike that had tears forming in both of our eyes. "No. You don't get to talk about her like that. Olivia is *not* second best. Not to me. I was falling for her well before I let go of my infatuation with you. She is *real*, not some fantasy. She's not some second choice. She's my *only* choice. Do you understand me?"

Taylor was crying as she nodded at me.

"I'm sorry," I said, reaching out and covering her hand with mine as she held her cheek.

"So am I."

"I still love you, you know. Just not...romantically. You're like a sister to me. Family." I took a deep breath. "Forgive me?"

She dropped her head. "I don't know how to deal with this. I'm so confused."

"Then start getting used to it, because I hope Olivia is in my life for a very, very long time."

Taylor nodded and I pulled her close. "I think Charli and I are over."

I sighed and hugged her tighter. I didn't know what to say to that. Letting Taylor go a little while later, I drew her in the direction of the house and froze. Olivia was standing there watching us. *How long had she been there?*

Taylor stiffened at my side. She muttered something about leaving us alone and tried to dash past Olivia. Olivia snatched her by the arm. "Are you okay?"

Taylor blinked with surprise. So did I. "Uh...yeah. I will be. Sorry about...you know...everything."

"You've nothing to apologize for, but I believe I do. I'm not trying to steal your best friend away. Yes, she's got smarts that will take her anywhere she wants to go, but if that means staying here, then I'm not going to protest it. She'll always have a choice. Besides, she's got several years left to fail, anyway. She might turn out to be hopeless." Olivia smiled and winked at me. I poked my tongue out at her.

Taylor smiled too and left after a nod of acceptance to Olivia.

"So," I said, walking up the steps to my girlfriend. "How much did you hear?"

"You slapped her."

I grimaced. That means she would have heard a lot. "Yeah. I kinda regret that."

"She was out of line."

I shrugged. Maybe so, but slapping my best friend...not part of my highlight reel. I huffed out a breath of air. "So you heard a lot then?"

"I did." Olivia stepped closer to me and wrapped her hands around my neck. "You surprise me."

"Good."

Olivia smiled and her eyes twinkled in the light from the porch. She studied me with those cool blue eyes until I began to fidget. "Happy birthday."

I blushed as she pressed a kiss to my cheek.

"Why didn't you tell me?"

"Umm...well...technically it's not my birthday until eight-thirty. We, uh, have this thing that we celebrate once my birth time comes."

"That's...different."

"It coincides with dessert. Thus the cheesecake I know you and Mom got earlier."

Olivia nodded.

"Umm...I know that...umm..." I bit my lip. How does one sensitively bring up someone else's dearly departed? "About your son." She stiffened instantly so I rushed through my explanation. "I know it's his birthday too. I'm sorry, I didn't mean to pry, but...I...I'm sorry, and, umm...yeah, happy birthday for him, too." I fidgeted and bit down hard on the inside of my cheek.

"Do you want to know why I'm specializing in pediatrics?"

I let out a rush of breath. "Yes."

Olivia took a deep breath. "Walk with me?"

It was a balmy evening and I guided her to the water's edge. Right to the place we once shared questions and answers in the winter chill. Sitting down on the pier side-by-side, she held my hand and stared over the lake as it shimmered under the moon.

"I was seventeen when I fell in love for the first time. Shamus was his name. An Irish boy that grew up around the corner from me. I got pregnant and wanted to make a go of having a family." She heaved in a breath of air and let it leak out. "Jayden was the name of our son. A beautiful boy born two weeks early...today. At five in the morning." Olivia smiled and my heart melted. "When he was born they noticed a congenital heart problem. Hypoplastic left heart syndrome."

I gasped. What a devastating diagnosis.

"He underwent surgery as soon as they deemed him strong enough, but..." Olivia shook her head. "Shamus and I didn't last. It was too much pressure and we were too young. Jayden...he was mine for ten months, and now...he's theirs." Olivia looked up at the stars. I leaned my head against her shoulder and silently studied the heavens with her. "I want to take care of children. To make them better and return them to their parents," she whispered.

"And you will," I whispered back as my heart ached for her. "You will."

"Why did you fight for me that night?" Olivia asked. Instinctively, I knew she meant the night she drank and raged at me.

"Because you were hurting. Because you needed me."

"I've never needed anyone," she said. "I've never had anyone stay. Never had anyone fight for me. Not the way you did that night. Not the way you did tonight with Taylor." She squeezed my hand and stared at me through the muted moonlight. "Are you sure?"

I screwed my brow up in confusion.

Olivia sighed. "That you want me. Are you sure that...I'm..."

"Worth it?"

Olivia nodded. "I'm not an easy person to like."

"I know."

"I'm not very nice most of the time."

"I know."

"I'm—"

"Everything I want," I said. She let out a rush of air. "Look, I know this is about to sound corny and probably stolen directly from a Sandra Bullock movie, but you complete me."

"That's Jerry Maguire, dear. Tom Cruise."

I smiled. "Whatever. Where I'm relaxed and incompetent, you're assertive and sure. Where I'm easy and uncomplicated, you're challenging and complex. Where I'm unorganized and random, you're controlled and dedicated. You're everything I'm not, but you're everything I need."

"You're right. It's corny."

"I know, right?" I chuckled and she joined me in quiet laughter under the waxing moon. "I know that relationships take work. But I'm ready to do that. Just…please don't shut me out. Okay?"

"I can't promise that, Darcy."

"I know," I whispered and squeezed her hand. I could tell that she was protected by layers of walls, and I figured there were a million reasons why. I just hoped that in time she'd let me peek behind the curtain and let me accept all of her. "I love you."

That earned me a sweet kiss. She leaned her forehead against mine. "I love you," she whispered back.

And together we stared at the stars and remained close. I smiled as the crickets chirped and the light twinkled on the surface of the lake. Music drifted from the house to the lake and warmed me like the woman at my side. This is where I belonged. This is where I wanted to be. And here, by Olivia's side, was where I would fight to remain. I wish I knew then just how much fighting I was going to have to do as the clinical years of Harvard Medical dawned.

###

Another Author's Note

Thank you for reading the first installment of the *Tricky Series*. The sequel *Tricky Chances* will be released in 2016. For now, feel free to leave a review, or find me on Facebook or Twitter @camryneyde, and at my website www.camryneyde.com.

Until next time, happy reading!

Camryn.

Other Books by Camryn Eyde

Romancing the Girl
Available in paperback and ebook

Aimee Turner is a country girl, living and working on her family's sheep station in rural Australia. Life is easy and full of hard, dusty work, but when her brother Joseph decides to become a contestant in a reality TV dating show, Romancing the Farmer, everything goes to hell.

The station gets overrun by city women and stuck-up producers right in the middle of shearing season. Justine Cason, the ringleader of the circus Aimee instantly detests is an irritating, arrogant presence that she is forced to chaperone around the massive property.

The two women find more in common than trading insults the more time they spend together, sparking an unexpected connection neither was looking for. As Joseph navigates the dating scene, and Aimee's sister Sally navigates a crumbling marriage, Aimee's life turns on its head in more ways than one when her blooming connection with Justine is the catalyst to leaving the land she loves.

When the worst fire season in decades strikes their patch of the world, the Turner family must find a way to save themselves and the ones they dearly cherish. Can they put aside their differences to protect each other?

The Woman Upstairs
Available in paperback and ebook

Ricci Velez is a fiercely independent woman that worked her way up from the poverty line to become a respected engineer and property developer. Mistaken as the little wifey by Tara Reeves, the new tenant at her Manhattan apartment building, Ricci wants to evict her before she even signs the lease. A slighted ex-tenant, a vandalized apartment, and an interfering best friend means that she's forced to offer Tara a room in her own apartment. Can she survive having the secretive hard-nosed executive judging her in her own home? Worse still, can she survive her match-making mother shamelessly besotted by the temporary housemate?

Made in the USA
Lexington, KY
07 April 2017